YOUNG
RANCH
DETECTIVE

CHARLES COOMBS

YOUNG
RANCH
DETECTIVE

ILLUSTRATED BY LOUIS PRISCILLA

JC 7744 yrd

LANTERN PRESS

NEW YORK

LIBRARY OF CONGRESS CATALOG NUMBER: 56-10011

PUBLISHED SIMULTANEOUSLY IN CANADA BY
GEORGE J. MC LEOD, LIMITED, TORONTO

MANUFACTURED IN THE UNITED STATES OF AMERICA

CONTENTS

ILLUSTRATIONS

CHAPTER ONE

Ned Bryant carried the black metal box carefully as he rode underneath a log archway and toward a nearby group of sun-baked ranch buildings. His freckled face was grimly serious. Somehow, he hoped the black box could solve the problems caused by the missing Rafter B cattle.

"Easy, Stormy," he coaxed his prancing black mustang. "These gadgets won't stand much bumping around."

He reined to a stop beside the rough-timbered ranch house. Before he had time to call out, the back screen door flew open. A taffy-haired girl ran out and stood smiling up at him. She wore a pink-and-white gingham dress. Her blue eyes sparkled.

"I was watching your trail dust, Ned," Julie Nelson said. "Sure glad you came over. We haven't played for nearly two weeks."

"I didn't come to play," Ned said. "The Rafter B is in trouble."

"Trouble?"

"We still can't locate some of our cattle, and—"

"We heard about it," Julie cut in. "My father is missing cattle, too. So are some of the other ranchers. But they will all turn up, I'm sure. There are lots of places for cattle to get lost in this open country."

"But they've never done it before," Ned insisted. "Not like now. So many are missing." He lifted his ten-gallon cowboy hat and brushed back the strands of dark reddish hair that had worked out from under the brim. With an end of the red bandanna knotted around his neck, he mopped the dusty sweat from his freckled face.

"Well, come on and get down," Julie

urged. "Stormy needs a rest. And I bet you could use a big glass of lemonade."

"Sure could," Ned said, slipping down to the ground. "But I can't stay long."

"Why not?" Julie asked. Then, for the first time, she noticed the black metal box slung over his shoulder. "You didn't need to bring your lunch, Ned," she added. "You know you're always welcome to eat here."

"Lunch?" Ned looked surprised. "I didn't bring any lunch. What makes you think—oh, I get it."

"Isn't that a lunch box?" Julie asked, pointing to the metal container. "But what are those wires sticking out of it?"

Ned laughed. "It's no lunch box, Julie. I thought everyone knew what a Geiger counter looks like."

"Is that a Geiger counter?" Julie asked, coming closer and touching the dark metal box. "Well, I've heard people talk about them, but this is the first time I've seen one. Where did you get it?"

"That Mr. Medford from the East gave it to us the other day."

"Gave it to you?"

"Yep. He said he was going back home. He said it was too hot in this part of the country for him. Besides, he couldn't seem to find any uranium. Said he didn't have any use for the Geiger counter any more. So he gave it to my dad and me for letting him use our water while he was prospecting."

"Well, I don't see why anyone would bother to come out here with a Geiger counter, anyway," Julie said. "There aren't any atom bombs to find around here."

"Atom bombs?" Ned said, laughing. "Julie, you don't hunt atom bombs with Geiger counters."

"Then what do you do with them?"

"You hunt for uranium, that's what," Ned explained. He wondered how anyone could know so little about the use of Geiger counters. People had been scouring the surrounding hills with them for months now. "You hunt for uranium, just like you hunt for gold."

"Well, I've seen lots of people hunt for

gold," Julie said. "But I've never seen any of them using a Geiger counter."

"That's different," Ned answered patiently. "You don't use a Geiger counter for gold. Gold isn't radioactive. Uranium is. It sends out invisible rays. When those rays reach the Geiger counter, they make something inside start clicking. When the clicks speed up real fast, you are close to uranium. It's that easy."

"Sounds easy, all right," Julie said. "But how do you know so much about Geiger counters, Ned?"

"I've been reading about them in magazines," Ned replied, "and I've talked with a few uranium hunters when they've come to the ranch to get water."

Julie walked along silently as Ned led his horse to the watering trough. Then she asked, "Are all of those people who have been running around here in jeeps and house trailers and everything looking for uranium?"

"Most of them are."

"Well, my father doesn't like it," Julie said. "They tramp or drive all over the country and scare the livestock."

"I know," Ned agreed. "But most of the land around here is owned by the government. Public land, they call it. And anyone can graze their cattle or—or hunt for gold or uranium or anything."

"Well," Julie said, "I hope they don't find any and go back home."

Ned smiled. "Maybe you're right," he said. "But old Tom Simpson found some way over on the other side of Mesa City. That's why there are so many people around hunting for more."

"Maybe there isn't any more."

"Maybe not," Ned admitted, "but if there is, I hope you and I are the ones to find it."

"Me and you?"

"Sure. Why do you think I brought the Geiger counter? I thought you might like to go prospecting with me."

Julie thought it over a minute. "Oh, Ned, that would be fun," she said eagerly.

"I'm not doing it for fun," Ned said seriously. "And if you think it's just a game—"

"All right, I take it back," Julie replied quickly, looking a little puzzled. "Anyway,

14

let's go ask my father if I can go with you. He's out by the barn."

They found Mr. Nelson beside the barn, tinkering with the ranch jeep with the Box N brand painted on the hood.

"So you have the fever, too, Ned," he said when the children had explained their plan. It seemed to Ned that Mr. Nelson spoke somewhat sternly. "I thought you Bryants were cattlemen, just like us Nelsons."

"Oh, we are, Mr. Nelson," Ned assured him. "Only—well, we've been having trouble with the cattle. Besides, if there is uranium around here, we have a better right to it than anyone."

"Depends on how you look at it, Ned," Mr. Nelson said. "Reckon those who find it have the real right to it. That's how it works on public lands. But you have a good point. If anyone really is entitled to find any uranium around here, it seems that we natives should be the ones. But from what I hear and read, you don't just go around picking up uranium in bushel baskets."

"Oh, no, sir," Ned said. "It's very hard to find. But with this Geiger counter—"

"Geiger counter?" Mr. Nelson asked. "I thought it was a shoe box or something."

Ned didn't miss the sly wink Mr. Nelson directed at Julie. "You're kidding me, Mr. Nelson," he accused. "You know what a Geiger counter is."

"Sure I do, Ned," Julie's father said, smiling. "Goodness knows, I've seen enough people tramping over the hills and through the sagebrush with them lately. Can't say I exactly enjoy seeing them, though. 'Fraid they're scaring the cattle out of the country. At least, something is. We're missing quite a few head." Mr. Nelson's face grew serious. "I understand the Rafter B is having the same trouble," he added.

"Yes, sir," Ned replied, nodding. "Quite a bunch of our steers seem to have disappeared."

"Cattle don't just disappear, Ned," the rancher said firmly. "There is always a mighty good reason for it. And unless we find that

16

reason pretty soon, and stop it, some of us cattlemen are going to be out of business."

The thought chilled Ned. Mr. Nelson was talking exactly the way his father had talked several times recently. At first, Ned had figured it was just a case of taking the time to hunt the cattle down. He thought they simply had grazed farther away than usual. Surely, in time they would all be located far up some canyon, or mixed in with some other herds.

That's what he had thought at first. But it was no longer that easy to explain. Not when most of the other ranchers also had missed cattle. Something was very wrong. Unless a solution was found soon, several of the ranches, including his father's Rafter B, would go broke.

"But you didn't ride all the way out here to talk about your troubles, or listen to mine," Mr. Nelson said. "If you and Julie figure to get any prospecting done today, you'd better be on your way. Don't go too far, and make it a point to be back by sundown."

"Oh, we'll be here before that, Mr. Nelson," Ned promised. "I've got to get back to the Rafter B in plenty of time to do my chores. Julie and I will just kind of scout around a little today. Of course, if we strike it rich, one of us had better stay to guard our treasure."

"That sounds sensible," Mr. Nelson said, smiling. "In the meantime, Julie, you'd better go check with your mother. Might be a good idea to take along a few sandwiches. And don't forget a canteen."

"I have my canteen, Mr. Nelson," Ned said.

"Good. Then I'll saddle up Calico for you, Julie."

Julie was gone longer than Ned had expected, but when she returned, wearing a pair of blue Levis and her riding boots, she carried a large brown paper sack.

"I know how hungry you always get, Ned," she explained, patting the sack. "All right. Let's go."

Soon they had ridden out of sight of the ranch buildings. More than once Ned was

18

tempted to challenge Julie to a short race. Ned's black mustang and Julie's pinto pony, Calico, were well matched as to speed. Seldom did Ned and Julie go riding together without a race. But today there were more serious thoughts on Ned's mind. No cattle ranch could earn money, or even keep running, unless it sent the proper number of steers to market. Since the Rafter B hadn't been able to find most of its steers, very few had gone to market. His father's face had become deeply lined with worry, and he had hinted strongly that they might have to move off the Rafter B.

Thinking about it now, Ned knew how important it was for him to discover some uranium. It seemed the only way to make up for the missing cattle.

The two young people had ridden about three miles from the ranch when they arrived at Wild Horse Canyon. Two jagged spires of rock marked the entrance to the broad and winding canyon. A small stream tumbled noisily over the boulders in the center of the valley. Walls of crumbling rock and shale

19

hemmed in the main canyon. At intervals, smaller arroyos and ravines forked off from either side.

"I haven't been out here since the roundup last spring," Julie said. "Usually we can locate quite a few head of cattle here in Wild Horse Canyon."

"Sure," Ned said. "That's because there's water and good grass. I haven't been out here, either, for at least a couple of months."

"But someone's been here," Julie remarked, pointing to the ground.

"I noticed those tire tracks," Ned answered, nodding. "They're pretty big ones, aren't they? Like truck tires. And it looks as though they've been back and forth quite a few times."

"Some people come out from Mesa City to picnic here," Julie said. "There are a lot of pretty places in the canyon."

"The tracks might have been made by uranium prospectors, too," Ned offered. "I've seen quite a few tire tracks while we've been riding. One thing about this country, you can

20

go almost anyplace in a car or jeep—roads or no roads."

"Let's ride up the canyon a ways," Julie suggested. "I know a place in the willows along the stream where we can have our lunch."

Ned took his canteen from the saddle horn. He unscrewed the cap and handed the water container over to Julie. "That's a good idea," he said. "We can fill the canteen again, too. After lunch we'll try out the Geiger counter. There are plenty of rocks along the edges of the canyon. Usually uranium is found in rocks. Anyway, it'll be worth trying."

After his own drink, Ned hung the canteen back around his saddle horn. They started out again. They rode slowly, for the noon sun blazed hot upon their backs. The shiny coats of the two horses were speckled with sweaty foam.

They were scarcely aware that the horses had automatically been following the tire tracks, which wove in and out between cactus, rocks, and sagebrush. As they rode around a mound of boulders and were heading for the group of willows which marked the bank of the stream, Stormy flicked his ears forward and nickered.

"He sees something," Ned said quickly.

"Maybe it's some of the lost cattle," Julie said hopefully.

"Well, let's have a look, anyway," Ned suggested. "Finding the cattle would be as good as finding uranium, and—"

"Stay right where you are!" a gruff voice commanded.

Startled, both Ned and Julie reined their horses to a jolting stop. It seemed that the voice had come from slightly above and to their right.

They turned their heads and saw the man at once. He was a large man. He stood spraddle-legged on top of a huge boulder. He was dressed in familiar Western garb—dark blue Levis, cowboy boots, and a faded blue shirt. A red bandanna was knotted around his neck.

From beneath the broad brim of his hat, the man's eyes scowled down at the two young people. There was a grimness on his unshaven

22

"Stay right where you are!" a gruff voice commanded.

face that sent a quick chill down Ned's spine.

"Stay right where you are!" the man repeated.

But the second warning was not necessary. Neither Ned nor Julie had any notion of riding on against the man's orders. For, cradled firmly in the big stranger's hands, was a very sinister-looking rifle.

And it was pointed right at Ned and Julie.

CHAPTER TWO

Ned looked into the barrel of the gun. He tried to voice some words of protest, but a strange lump in his throat blocked them off. He had seen quite a few guns in his twelve years, but this was the first time one had been pointed at him. It was a frightening sensation. His discomfort increased when he saw that the man's finger rested nervously on the trigger.

"Don't—don't you dare shoot, mister!" Julie was the first to find her voice. "We haven't done anything."

"We—we have a right to be out here just as much as you do." Ned managed at last to speak around the lump in his throat. Even to himself, his voice sounded squeaky with excitement and fright.

A slight smile played across the man's whiskery face. Slowly he lowered the barrel of the rifle, and stepped down toward the two young riders.

"Why, you're just a couple of kids, ain't you," he said, squinting out from the shadows beneath his broad-brimmed hat.

"Well, we're not so little," Ned defended. He felt a little braver without the gun pointed at him. "And—and you better leave us alone. This is government land. You don't own it. We have as much right to be here as anyone."

"Well, now," the dark stranger said slowly, "maybe you're right, at that. But what are you doin' out here, anyway?"

"We're uranium hunters," Julie answered quickly.

"You are?" the man said with mild surprise. "That's mighty interestin'. Find any?"

"Not yet," Ned said. "We haven't even had a chance to switch on our Geiger counter. But when we do—"

"Oh, a Geiger counter, eh?" the man said. "Say, that's a pretty touchy gadget for just a couple of punk kids to be monkeyin' around with, ain't it?"

"I know how to use it," Ned said firmly. He didn't like the man's manner. There was no point in anyone being so unfriendly. Ned had met a lot of prospectors, cowboys, and just plain tourists during the years he had lived in the West, but never had any of them pointed a gun at him before and never had they spoken in quite the mean tone of voice this man was using.

"Well, I reckon you better be takin' it someplace else," the stranger said. "This happens to be our territory. We don't want anyone snooping around."

"We?" Julie asked. "Who's 'we'?"

Julie could have saved the question. Even as she spoke, Ned's eyes were focusing on a strange sight. Beyond them a few hundred feet was a large truck. It was half hidden in a thick clump of willows. It was dusty-brown and boxlike. It looked almost as big as some of the moving vans Ned had seen around Mesa City.

27

Near it a thin trickle of gray smoke marked the remains of a campfire. For the first time Ned saw two other men walking toward them.

"Look," Julie said, also catching sight of the men.

"Yeah, I see," Ned said. "What's the truck for, mister?"

"None of your business," the man said gruffly. Then he seemed to think better of his manners. "Mean to tell me you've never seen people out campin' before?"

Ned didn't answer, but he didn't think it was a very good explanation of what the men were doing there. If it was a camping outfit, it was the strangest one he ever had seen. Besides, what kind of a camper would aim a rifle at him and Julie?

"Who you got there, Brock?" a tall, thin man called as the strangers drew closer.

"Just a couple of kids," the man called Brock replied. "Reckon they're harmless, though."

By then all of the men were gathered in front of Ned and Julie. They talked among

28

themselves, in low voices. Ned couldn't hear what they were saying.

Finally the three men stopped talking. They seemed more at ease as they turned to Ned and Julie, still astride the horses. "Well," the man called Brock said, "I hope I didn't scare you kids. But, you know how it is—us uranium prospectors have to be kind of careful about who comes snoopin' around our claims."

"Oh," Julie said quickly, "are you hunting for uranium, too?"

"Sure 'nuff," Brock answered. "Ain't that what everyone's doin' around here these days?" He smiled lopsidedly.

"Just about everyone, I guess," Ned said. But he didn't feel completely sure that these three men were also uranium prospectors. There was something about the twisted smile on Brock's face that didn't quite set right. "If you're uranium hunters, where are your Geiger counters?" Ned spoke the thought in his mind.

"Oh, you don't believe us, huh?" Brock

said. "Well, we've got one, all right. Fact is, Tabor and Slim and I have quite an outfit. Can't show it to you, though. You know how it is. Secret stuff. Doesn't do to tell everybody your business. Right, Slim? Right, Tabor?"

The tall, blond-haired man called Slim smiled thinly, showing crooked rows of tobacco-stained teeth. "That's right, Brock," he said. "You can't get rich when you go blabbing to everybody about what you're doing."

"Is that why you keep your truck and stuff hidden in the trees?" Julie asked.

"You have mighty big eyes, haven't you, young one?" the man called Tabor said. He was a squat fellow with a short, bull-like neck and an almost entirely hairless head. The stub of a cold cigar dangled from the corner of his mouth. The heat seemed to bother him more than it did the other two. His pudgy face glistened with perspiration. "And just what's wrong with keeping our outfit under the trees?"

"N-nothing, I guess," Julie said.

"Where you kids from?" Brock asked.

For a moment Ned considered giving them

some false information. Then he wondered why he felt that way. After all, there had been quite a few uranium prospectors in and out of the area. Most of those he had seen were friendly people. He had enjoyed listening to them and visiting with them. He wondered why he had a different feeling toward these three men. Perhaps it was because they were gruff and rough-looking. Perhaps it was that they had such a big outfit, and seemed to want to keep it hidden. Besides, most prospectors liked to talk about their work and adventures. Of course, those Ned had met hadn't found any uranium ore, so talk couldn't hurt anything.

He wondered now if these three men had found uranium. Perhaps that was the reason they didn't seem pleased at having him and Julie around. Well, that was their business. You could hardly blame them. Anyway, it was no reason for him not to answer their question about where he and Julie were from.

"I'm from the Rafter B Ranch," Ned said proudly. "And Julie is from the Box N."

The three men glanced quickly at each other.

"Oh, you're cattle ranchers," Brock said. "I thought you said you were uranium prospectors?"

"Well, we are," Ned said. "Right now, anyway. Besides, while we're looking for uranium, we might even run across some of our missing cattle."

"Missing cattle?" Slim asked.

"Sometimes the steers wander away and get lost," Ned explained. "It's not always easy to find them."

"And there seem to be an awful lot of them missing this year," Julie added.

"Maybe you should put bells on 'em," the chunky man, Tabor, suggested with a smile.

"Bells or no bells, we ain't seen none around here," Brock said. "No uranium, either. So you kids better be movin' on. We've got work to do."

"I'd sure like to see your outfit," Ned said. "It looks mighty big. You must have a lot of equipment. I've never seen uranium prospectors with such a big truck as that."

"Well, we ain't goin' to show it to you," Brock said gruffly. "Prospectin' is secret work. But I tell you what we'll do. If you don't tell anybody we're out here prospectin', we won't tell anyone that you are. That way, when one of us locates a good uranium mine, we won't have everybody and his brother rushin' out here to stake a claim. How's that?"

Ned didn't answer. He couldn't see any reason for keeping everything such a secret. After all, Brock had just admitted that they hadn't found any uranium. If that were true, why hadn't they simply packed up their equipment and moved on to some other territory? There were several things about these men that Ned didn't understand.

"Let's go, Ned," Julie spoke up. "Time's wasting. We want to get some use out of your Geiger counter before we have to start back to the ranch."

"Guess you're right," Ned said. "And, Mr. Brock, if you happen to run across any cattle out here, we sure would appreciate it if you'd drop by the Rafter B or the Box N and let our fathers know."

33

"Sure, kid. But I don't think there are any around here," Brock said. "At least, we ain't seen signs of none."

"That's right," Slim said quickly. "But if we see any, we sure will let you know. Now you better beat it. Pronto."

"You don't need to talk to them like that, Slim," Tabor scolded. "These kids are our friends. Ain't you, kids?"

"I—I guess so," Ned said. But he certainly didn't feel very much as though these men were his friends. He turned to lead the way back toward the mouth of the canyon, but Stormy resisted the pressure of the reins. Instead, the mustang suddenly arched his neck, flicked his ears forward, and looked alertly toward a mound of large rocks a couple of hundred feet away. Stormy nickered and pawed at the ground with his sharp hoofs.

Ned heard the faint sound of a returning whinny.

"I didn't know you men had horses, too," Ned said.

"What makes you think we have?" Slim asked sharply.

34

"That sure sounded like a horse whinnying," Ned said.

"I didn't hear nothing," Tabor said. "Maybe you just heard a wild burro or something. Lot of them around here, you know."

"Do burros sound like horses?" Julie asked, and Ned realized that she also had heard it.

Ned said, "Let's go, Julie. We've got some prospecting to do." He spoke quickly, and he tried not to notice the close looks the men were giving him.

Without saying good-by to the three men, Ned and Julie reined their horses around and rode back down the canyon.

"They sure weren't very friendly, were they?" Julie said, once they were well out of earshot.

"I've never seen prospectors just like them before," Ned answered, puzzled. "And why would they want to lie to us? We weren't going to try stealing their uranium or anything."

"What do you mean lie, Ned?" Julie asked. "They didn't have to tell us the truth about whether they had really found any uranium or

35

not. Prospectors don't usually talk about such things."

"I don't mean that," Ned said. "It doesn't matter to me whether they have found uranium or not. But why did they want to deny that there was a horse over behind those rocks?"

"Maybe it was a burro, just like they said," Julie offered. "Maybe we just didn't hear right."

"Hey, you know better than that," Ned scolded. "Burros bray, and they don't sound anything like a horse. That was a horse, sure as shooting. And if those fellows have horses, what's the point in trying to keep it a secret?"

"I don't know, Ned," Julie admitted. "But I don't think I've seen or heard more than two wild burros in the years we've lived here. I didn't think there were many around."

"There aren't," Ned said. "And even if there was one, it wouldn't be hanging around that close to camp. They're really wild."

"Then why do you suppose that man called Tabor said it was a burro?"

"That's what I'd like to know," Ned replied. "But that's only one thing that doesn't figure out right."

"You mean you think they lied about something else?" Julie wanted to know.

"I sure do," Ned said firmly. "Remember, they said they hadn't seen any cattle around there?"

"Yes, I remember."

"Then what do you suppose made all of those steer tracks on the ground around us?"

"I didn't notice any tracks," Julie said.

"Well, I sure did. Quite a lot of them, too."

"That doesn't really mean anything, though, Ned," Julie said. "They might have been there a long time, for all we know."

"I know fresh cattle tracks when I see them," Ned insisted. "And those tracks weren't over a couple of days old."

"Well, maybe those men came in there within the last day or two," Julie suggested. "In fact, maybe they're what scared the cattle away."

Ned shrugged and sighed. "You might be

37

right, Julie," he admitted. "Maybe just because those guys acted funny-like I've been
imagining things."

"Sure you have, Ned," Julie said, smiling.
"Now, come on. Let's do some hunting with
that Geiger counter. I want to see how it
works."

"O.K.," Ned said. "But let's get out of this
canyon first. We can go over by the rimrock
along the mesa. We can try the Geiger counter
out there. First, though, what do you say we
eat? I'm getting mighty hungry."

"Now you're talking," Julie agreed cheer-
fully. "Let's just forget about those men.
Come on. I'll race you to the foot of the rimrock."

"It's a go," Ned said. He leaned forward in
the saddle. Stormy broke into a gallop.

But, as he and Julie raced out of Wild
Horse Canyon and toward the towering rimrock, it was not easy for Ned to erase from
his mind the actions of the three strangers.

CHAPTER THREE

Ned and Julie were soon eating their picnic lunch under a large spreading ironwood tree. Ned was deep in thought, trying to unscramble the strange actions and words of the three men they had just met in Wild Horse Canyon. He wished he had been able to get a closer look at the truck van. He hadn't noticed any windows in it, and he didn't think it was used to live in. On the other hand, prospectors didn't usually carry much equipment. So why would they need such a big truck?

"Boy, those were good sandwiches, Julie,"

he said after a while. "The deviled eggs, too. Thanks a lot." He rose and walked over to the patch of dry grass where the horses were grazing.

"Why don't we just leave Stormy and Calico here?" Julie called to him. "Wouldn't it be easier to use the Geiger counter if we're walking? It's just a short hike over to the foot of the rimrock, anyway."

"Good idea, Julie," Ned agreed. He got the leather hobbles out of the saddlebags. He fastened them around the horses' forefeet. The hobbles would allow Stormy and Calico to move around to graze, but would keep them from wandering too far away while Ned and Julie were gone. Ned also removed the saddles, so the horses would be more comfortable.

"Guess we're all set," he said finally. They started off across the sage- and cactus-studded dry wash. The ground became more rocky near the low but steep bluff that rimmed the wash. Ned stopped and put the earphones over his head.

"We might as well see what the background count is," he announced.

"Background count?" Julie asked. "What's that?"

"Well," Ned explained, "the Geiger counter clicks whenever you turn it on. Doesn't matter whether you're near uranium or not. Only if there's no uranium it clicks slowly."

"But you said when it clicks that's how you find uranium," Julie said.

"Only when it clicks fast," Ned insisted. "Most all rocks have a tiny bit of radioactivity in them. And also the cosmic rays in the air make the counter click a little. So you get some clicking no matter where you are." He flicked the switch on the metal box which hung from the strap around his shoulder. He listened to the slow clicking through the earphones.

"Here," he said, taking the set off and handing it to Julie. "Listen."

Julie held the phones to her ears. "I hear it," she said excitedly. "Click, click, click."

"Kind of remember how close those clicks are together," Ned said. "Then, later, we'll see if they get a lot faster."

"Oh, Ned, this is fun!" Julie exclaimed.

"Well, it's not supposed to be just a game," Ned said, reaching for the earphones.

"I didn't mean it that way," Julie said indignantly. "But you don't have to be so awfully serious, do you?"

Ned started to argue, then thought better of it. What was the object of trying to make Julie understand how important it was to find uranium? Something had to be done to make up for the Rafter B losing so many cattle. Ned loved ranch life. He didn't want to have to leave. Uranium was very valuable. So, if he could just find a little of it—well, it would at least furnish the money needed to run the ranch until the cattle were located or a new herd started.

But there wasn't much point in trying to explain it all to Julie. If she didn't realize that her own Box N Ranch was also in trouble, he wasn't going to be the one to worry her.

Ned used the Geiger counter sparingly. He wanted to save the batteries as much as possible. It was only when they reached a mound of likely-looking rocks that he paused, switched on the counter, and listened through the earphones.

"Any uranium?" Julie asked each time they stopped.

But each time Ned shook his head, switched off the counter, and moved on. At one spot the counter speeded up its clicking a little, but Ned remembered that Mr. Medford had said if there was uranium around the counter would click so rapidly it would sound like eggs frying in a hot skillet. Nowhere did he hear anything that sounded like frying eggs.

As the afternoon wore on there was really nothing very encouraging about the way the Geiger counter acted. Julie wandered away to inspect cactus flowers or to chase lizards. Even Ned began to lose interest in the monotonous slow clicking of the counter, so when Julie suggested that they start back toward the horses, he didn't argue.

"Only thing is," Ned said, "we're so near the top of the bluff, let's go on up and see the view of the canyon from the edge of the rim-rock. Might be able to spot some good-looking uranium spots, even."

43

"Oh, all right, if you want to," Julie agreed. She gazed upward wearily and measured the remaining distance to the top. "Only there's just the mesa. I've seen it before." But she trailed along as Ned climbed upward through the jumble of loose shale that centuries of wind and rain had broken free from the layer of cap rock and toppled down the steeply slanting bluff.

By the time they reached the mesa, both were puffing hard. Ned paused on top to mop his face.

"Boy, that's some sight," he said, with a wide sweep of his arm to indicate the valley that lay below. "Uranium or no uranium, we're sure lucky to be living out here, Julie."

"Oh, I know, Ned," his companion agreed. "I like it, too. I always have. My father calls it elbow room. He says everyone needs elbow room. And out West here is the best place to get it. Hey, look, you can even see those three men's camp from here."

"Where?"

"Over there to the left," Julie said, pointing. "Just beyond the top of that low hill

44

separating Wild Horse Canyon from the dry wash. See?"

"Oh, yeah," Ned said, shielding his eyes from the sun. He was barely able to make out the brown cube of the truck half hidden in the trees. "Boy, wish we had a pair of field glasses."

"Ned, you wouldn't snoop, would you?"

"Why not?" Ned said. "I'd sure like to know more about those fellows."

"Well, I wouldn't," Julie insisted. "I didn't like the way they acted. They can have their old uranium."

"Maybe you're right," Ned said. "But I'm not so sure they were telling us the truth about the uranium. Something about them seems awful fishy to me."

"Well, for goodness sakes, don't let it bother you, Ned," Julie scolded. "We can do very well without them."

"O.K., O.K.," Ned said, turning around to gaze across the mesa. "But I'd still— Hey, do you see what I see?"

Julie turned and looked in the direction Ned was pointing. The flat top of the mesa stretched back from the edge of the rimrock for as far as the eye could see.

"You mean that cloud of dust?" Julie asked.

"Yeah, but look what's making the dust," Ned prompted. "If those aren't sheep I'll eat my saddlebags." There was a sharp note of anger in his voice.

"Now don't go getting mad, Ned," Julie cautioned quickly.

But the warning was left unheeded. The sheepmen had always been a sore subject to the cattlemen. The cattle ranchers had no legal right to drive the herdsmen off the land, but cattlemen seldom missed the chance to make the sheepmen feel unwelcome. The browsing flocks of sheep nibbled the grass right down to the very roots. In fact, often they even pulled up the roots, or cut the ground to pieces with their sharp hoofs. Where sheep had been, there was little forage left for cattle.

Sheepherders and cattlemen had been bitter rivals from early frontier days. Once in a while, efforts were made between the two groups to work out their problems in friendly

46

fashion, but the long-standing rivalry for grass always seemed to return. And with it returned bitterness.

Now, along with his other problems, the feeling of rivalry surged up strong in Ned.

"Come on," he said. "Let's go see who those sheep belong to."

"Oh, Ned," Julie protested, "there's nothing you can do about it. This is open range."

"Well, I can sure let him know that he and his sheep aren't wanted around here," Ned said stubbornly. "We cattlemen were here first. And those sheep might be the big reason why our cattle have been so hard to find. Cattle don't like the smell of sheep. They go away when sheep are around."

Ned didn't wait for Julie's reply. He strode quickly across the mesa toward the browsing flock. Once again Julie silently fell into step behind him.

When they were still a couple of hundred yards from the sheep, a black and white dog separated itself from the flock and raced toward them. It barked a loud warning as it came.

47

"That looks like Manuel Machado's dog."

"That looks like Manuel Machado's dog," Julie said. "Ned, he looks ferocious. He might bite—"

"He better not try it," Ned said, reaching for a stick.

Just then a shrill whistle echoed across the mesa from the direction of the close-packed flock. Almost as though he had a rope tied to his neck, the dog quickly froze in his tracks. He kept his dark eyes on the two young people, but didn't move any closer. He stopped barking, but a growl rumbled deep in his throat.

The owner of the whistle soon appeared out of the haze of dust that hung over the flock. He trotted across the mesa toward Julie and Ned. The two young people stood still, not wanting to invite any further attack from the dog.

"That sure looks like Manuel Machado," Julie exclaimed. "I haven't seen him since school let out."

"It's Manuel, all right," Ned said, as the running figure drew closer.

"Down, Chico!" the Mexican boy com-

49

manded, as he approached Ned and Julie. The black and white sheepdog dropped obediently to the ground. "Hey, Ned and Julie, my friends, I didn't know it was you."

"It's us all right," Ned said, glaring at the small, bronze-skinned Mexican boy. "But what makes you think we're your friends?"

Manuel Machado's white teeth disappeared as the smile left his face.

"Ned doesn't mean that, Manuel," Julie said, scowling at Ned.

But Ned had his own feelings about what he meant or didn't mean. A sheepherder was a sheepherder. It didn't matter whether he was a schoolmate or not. Beneath the shadow of his wide-brimmed straw hat, Manuel struggled to recapture his smile.

"Chico," the Mexican boy turned to his dog, "go watch the sheep." He made a sweeping gesture with his arm. The dog immediately raced off in the direction of the grazing flock.

"He sure minds you," Julie said admiringly.

"Chico is a good dog," Manuel said proudly. He spoke excellent English, as did most of the Mexican and Indian children who went to the public school in Mesa City. "What have you two been doing since school let out?"

"Right now we're hunting for uranium," Julie answered, almost feeling Ned's scowl.

"And we're also hunting for the cattle that your sheep have chased off the range," Ned accused.

"Sheep don't chase cattle, Ned," Manuel said with mild surprise.

"You know good and well what I mean," Ned insisted. "The way those sheep smell and tear up the range—well, no steer wants to stay around."

"That's not true, Ned," Manuel argued. "The sheep and the cattle get along all right together. It just seems to be the sheepmen and the cattlemen who don't. Why is that, Ned?"

"You know as well as I do, Manuel," Ned said curtly.

"No, I don't. Not really," the Mexican boy insisted. "Oh, sure, I've heard lots of stories, just like you. But it's mostly not true, Ned."

"That's what you think."

51

"Then how come I've been seeing some cattle around here during the past few days?" Manuel wondered.

"You have?" Julie asked eagerly. "You mean Rafter B and Box N cattle?"

"I never got close enough to see their brands," Manuel said. "But you should know who they belong to. A couple of cowboys were driving them. They must be from one of your ranches."

Ned looked at Julie. "Has your father been out looking for cattle during the past few days?" he asked.

"No, I'm sure he hasn't," Julie said, puzzled. "He has stayed right around the ranch."

"So has my dad," Ned said. "In fact, no one I know of has been out trying to round up cattle during the past week. There has been so much ranch work to do."

"But," Manuel said, "they might not even have been your cattle."

"That's possible," Julie admitted, "but most of the cattle in this territory belong either to the Rafter B or the Box N. The other ranchers graze their stock on the other side of the hills."

Ned had been so concerned over Manuel's mention of seeing the cattle that he had almost forgotten his ill feeling toward the young Mexican sheepherder. Now his resentment returned, as he accepted the idea that the cattle might have belonged to some other spread. Otherwise, why would men be driving them?

"How long do you figure to be fattening up your sheep off our cattle range?" Ned asked sharply.

"It's not your range, Ned," the Mexican boy reminded him truthfully. "If this were your land, I wouldn't be here. But this is all open range, Ned. And you know it. I can stay here as long as I want. Sheep have to eat, you know. But if it will make you happy to know it, I plan to start grazing the flock back toward Mesa City soon. They're pretty fat now. Besides, they're due to be shipped out in about two weeks. I just hope I don't have any more accidents with them."

"Accidents?" Julie asked. "What kind of

53

accidents, Manuel? You mean coyotes, or mountain lions, or something?"

"Not coyotes or mountain lions," Manuel said. "A truck—at least, I think it was a truck —ran into some of them. Right out on the open range, too. Not a road for miles around."

"That sounds crazy," Ned said. "How could anything run into your sheep out on the open range?"

"Sounds crazy to me, too," Julie agreed. "How could anyone run into your sheep without seeing them?"

"It was at night," Manuel said.

"A truck ran into your sheep at night?" Ned exclaimed, laughing. "You've sure been having nightmares, fellow."

"Nightmares don't kill two sheep and injure six others," Manuel said firmly.

"He must be telling the truth, Ned," Julie said. "That's awful, Manuel. But I suppose the driver paid for the damage, didn't he?"

"Pay?" Manuel said angrily. "He didn't even stop."

"What kind of a truck was it?" Ned asked,

convinced that the Mexican herder was telling the truth.

"I didn't really see that it was a truck," Manuel answered. "It was real dark and I was in my bedroll. I saw its lights, though. And in the morning I saw the tire tracks. They were big. That's why I think it was a truck. I've been seeing quite a lot of those tracks."

"You have? Where?" Ned demanded. He wasn't sure just why he was suddenly so interested. But he hated the thought of any animals being mistreated or injured. His feelings even included sheep. Besides, it was certainly unusual that a truck would be driving around the roadless country at night.

"Oh," Manuel said, "I've seen the tracks crisscrossing the mesa quite often. I have even seen them going along the bottoms of a couple arroyos."

"You mean the tracks of that one truck?" Ned asked.

"Well, if it is a truck, I can't be sure it's the same one making all the tracks," Manuel admitted, "but I think so."

55

"There's nothing so unusual about that," Julie put in. "After all, uranium hunters have been tearing all over the countryside for months. I've seen them in cars, jeeps, trucks, and about everything else. But I still can't imagine anyone running into some of your sheep without even stopping to help, or offering to pay for the damage."

"They won't get away with it for long," Manuel said. "I think that same outfit has been heading for Mesa City every couple of nights. I've heard it. You know how far sound carries out here at night. I've even seen its lights a couple of times."

"What do you think it means, Manuel?" Ned asked.

The young sheepherder seemed a bit surprised at Ned's sudden show of interest and his friendlier tone. "I just don't know why a truck or anything else would be running around out here at night," the Mexican boy said simply. "But one of these nights it will pass by close enough for me to get a good look at it. When it does, and when I get back to

56

Mesa City—boy, the sheriff sure will hear about it in a hurry."

"Have you ever seen it in the daytime?" Julie asked.

"Not once," Manuel said. "It's just as though it disappears and, like an owl, comes out only at night."

"Ned," Julie said, looking at the sky, "the sun's getting low. If we don't hurry, we won't get any more uranium prospecting done today."

Ned realized then that Manuel's strange experience with the night-prowling truck had caused his thoughts to wander away from the original purpose of their ride.

"It's a long walk back to your ranches," Manuel said.

"Oh, we have our horses hobbled over at the foot of the bluff," Julie explained. "It's easier to hunt uranium on foot."

"This is the closest I've ever been to a Geiger counter," Manuel said, looking with eager interest at the metal box hanging at Ned's side. "I've only seen pictures of them in magazines."

57

By that time some of Ned's feeling of distaste for the sheepherder had begun to return. Instead of inviting the Mexican boy to have a closer look at the Geiger counter, he turned on his heel and started away. "Come on, Julie," he said over his shoulder. "We've got to be going."

He was tempted to give Manuel another warning about getting his sheep out of the territory as quickly as he could. He wanted to lay claim to what grass was left. But Manuel seemed to know his rights. He certainly didn't bluff or scare easily. Ned realized there wasn't a thing he could do about the Mexican sheepherder being there, or about trying to force him to leave.

"We don't need all the grass, anyway," Julie said, as though reading his thoughts. "We— we won't even need any grass if we can't find some of our cattle to eat it."

Ned didn't answer, but Julie was right, of course. The thought was a grim one, and a mysterious one. Already it had taken much of his attention away from the uranium hunt.

In fact, as he and Julie made their way back toward the waiting horses, Ned didn't even bother to switch on the Geiger counter.

CHAPTER FOUR

During the next few days Ned had no chance to take the Geiger counter out of the ranch house. He helped his father mend fence. He busied himself taking care of the few head of cattle that had been rounded up. There were other chores needing to be done.

One day word reached the ranch that a second rich uranium discovery had been located out by Twin Peaks. Ned wondered if the three men he and Julie had happened across in Wild Horse Canyon had been the ones to make the discovery. Twin Peaks was fairly near to the canyon, and the men in the strange vanlike truck probably did a lot of moving around.

Ned had thought of those men quite a few times. He thought of the gruff and strange manner in which they had treated him and Julie. But he never spoke of the meeting to his father. After all, his father had plenty of other things on his mind. He wasn't likely to be interested in three men who simply didn't act the way you might expect them to.

Then, a couple of days after word of the new discovery got around, Ned looked up from his garden hoeing to see Julie riding toward him on Calico.

"What happened to you, Ned?" she asked, reining to a stop. "I thought we were going to do some more uranium prospecting."

"I've been busy helping Dad," Ned explained. "I don't know when I'll be able to go uranium hunting again."

"Oh," Julie said, plucking at the rawhide tie string on her saddle, "I—I hoped maybe we could try it again—right away."

"Why right away?" Ned asked. He hadn't

given up entirely his hope to discover uranium. It still seemed the best way to make up for the missing cattle. But their lack of success the one day they had gone searching certainly had discouraged him.

"Ned, it's—it's real important," Julie said urgently.

"Hey," Ned said, looking at her closely. The usual cheerful sparkle was missing from Julie's blue eyes. "Something's the matter, Julie. Why are you looking so—so worried?"

"Ned, it's awful!" Julie blurted. Her lower lip trembled.

"What's awful? Come on. Get down and tell me. No secrets."

Julie slid out of her saddle. Ned took the reins and led Calico over to the barn. He removed the bridle and saddle, and put the pinto in an empty stall. He knew Julie had something important on her mind, but he wanted to hear the story all in one piece. When he had finished taking care of Calico, he said, "Let's go out under the cottonwoods behind the barn. We can talk better there."

Soon they were settled in the shade. Julie

63

plucked a spear of grass and began to chew on it.

"Tell me," Ned urged. "What's wrong?"

"We—we've just got to find some uranium, Ned," Julie said tensely.

"Well, we can at least try again, I guess," Ned said. He was puzzled, though, over Julie's sudden interest in finding uranium. She had seemed to tire of the hunt rather quickly the one time they had gone out. "One of these days when I have my chores all caught up—"

"One of these days may be too late," Julie said.

"But why?" Ned asked. "Whatever uranium is around here has been here for millions of years. A few days won't make much difference in finding it."

"Oh, but a few days might make a lot of difference, Ned."

"What do you mean?"

"We—we may not be here," Julie blurted out.

"I'm not figuring to go anyplace," Ned said.

"I don't mean that, Ned," Julie said. "I

64

mean my parents and I may be gone. The Box N may belong to someone else."

Then Julie told Ned the entire story. The missing Box N cattle simply had not been found. At first, Mr. Nelson, like Ned's own father, had thought the cattle must have grazed farther away from the home range than usual. During the last week he had visited several of the outlying ranches. He had scouted far out into the isolated canyons where the cattle had never been known to go before. He had located only a few head. The other ranchers reported seeing no steers bearing the Box N brand.

Mr. Nelson had returned home deeply worried, Julie said. She had seen it written plainly on her father's face, although he had tried to hide it from her.

"Then, last night," Julie went on, "I couldn't get to sleep. I heard Mother and Daddy talking in the kitchen quite late. Daddy said something about the bank in Mesa City having no choice."

"No choice about what?" Ned asked.

"About taking the ranch."

"Taking the ranch? How could the bank do that?"

"Daddy borrowed money from the bank so we could go into the cattle business," Julie explained. "He has to make regular monthly payments to the bank. If he doesn't make the payments on the loan, then the bank can actually take the ranch. They own a mortgage. They can sell the ranch to someone else in order to get their money back."

"Aw, they wouldn't do that," Ned assured her. "Mr. Leland at the bank is a good friend of your dad's. He's a friend of ours, too."

"I know," Julie said, nodding. "But that doesn't matter. When you borrow money, you must pay it back. That is business—friends or no friends. I heard my folks talking about that. Mr. Leland can't help it. He doesn't actually own the bank. He just runs it."

"I see," Ned said thoughtfully. "With no cattle to sell, your father can't make the payments on the loan, and he loses the ranch. Is that it?"

"Exactly," Julie said. "That's exactly it."

66

Ned didn't say anything else for a minute. He wondered if it was the same way with the Rafter B. His father had never said anything about owing money to the bank, but he had mentioned several times recently that the ranch wasn't paying its own way. Ned didn't know much about money matters, but he certainly knew that no ranch could keep going if it was losing money. That was as simple as A, B, C. Now it occurred to him that nothing could be worse than to have the Rafter B lose money. Nothing could be worse than having to move off the ranch.

Ned decided that he would ask his father all about the situation as soon as he had a chance. But right now Julie had made it very clear why she had become so interested in another uranium hunt.

"If—if we could just find a little of it," she said, "at least it might help Daddy to keep from losing the ranch until our cattle are found or—or until we can get a new herd started."

"I don't see how the cattle can be found if your father has hunted all the places you say,"

Ned said, shaking his head. "But cattle don't just disappear, either," he added, remembering that his father had said the same thing some time back. "I just can't savvy it."

"Neither can I," Julie agreed. "But they're gone, and we've got to do something."

Ned saw that she was near tears again. "Sure, Julie," he said, touching her gently on the arm. "We'll do something. Just don't worry."

Julie smiled faintly. "You're a real good friend, Ned," she murmured.

"Well," he said honestly, "I'm doing it for the Rafter B, too, you know. We've lost a lot of cattle, too."

"I know, Ned. Can we go today? It's still early."

"I'll ask my dad," Ned said. "But I only hope we'll have better luck than we did last week."

"We didn't look very hard," Julie reminded him. "Meeting those three men, and then talking to Manuel Machado—well, it didn't leave us much time really to look for uranium."

68

"That's so," Ned admitted.

"Besides," Julie said, attempting to be cheerful, "I know more about it now. I've been reading those articles in the Mesa City *Roadrunner* about uranium prospecting."

"That should make it a cinch to find some," Ned said, laughing. "Did it tell you exactly where to dig? Maybe we don't even need to take the Geiger counter."

"I didn't mean that I'm an expert," Julie said, pouting slightly. "But I didn't want to be so dumb about it. I even clipped a map of some of the best places around here to hunt for uranium. Some of them are quite near. Please go ask your father if you can go, Ned. We should get started."

After getting his father's permission, Ned saddled up Stormy and Calico. He and Julie started out.

"Can I see the map a minute, Julie?" Ned asked after they had ridden about fifteen minutes.

Julie pulled the map out of one of her saddlebags and handed it over to her companion. They stopped in the shade of a scrub

69

oak. Ned studied the map. He noted the places marked as possible uranium sites.

"Of course, they're only guesses," Julie admitted. "But some people—I think they are called geologists—can tell quite a bit about where uranium is most likely to be found. They've studied all about rock formations and stuff."

"Yeah, I know," Ned said. "Funny, though, that they are so willing to tell everyone about it. Even put it on maps like this. You'd think they would dig it themselves."

"You still have to find it, though, maps or no maps," Julie said. "And that can be a mighty hard job."

Ned smiled. "You can say that again. Look at all the people who have been around here hunting it. And I've heard of only two people who found any."

"Well, if two found it, others can. There must be more of it around," Julie said. "But, Ned, why is uranium so important? I don't like the idea of every time someone finds more uranium it means more atom bombs. I don't like atom bombs, Ned."

70

"Who does? But they're not using it for atom bombs much any more," Ned assured her. "They're using it more for curing diseases, and for making electricity, and running machinery, and things like that. They get energy out of uranium, just like they do out of coal."

"What do you mean, energy?"

"Well, the energy from coal is heat," Ned explained. He had to think hard to remember some of the things he had read recently. "Heat can run trains or steamships or airplanes—and things like that. It can run electric generators, too."

"In school I read that electric generators are run by water," Julie said. "They make electricity out at Squaw Dam."

"Well, that's right," Ned admitted. "The weight of the water is a form of energy. When it spurts out from behind a dam with a lot of pressure it can turn great enormous wheels—wheels like the rotors in electricity generators. But there's another way, too. You can heat water to make steam. And that steam can run the generators. That's where coal comes

71

in mighty handy. They use it to heat the water to make the steam to run the generators, or lots of other kinds of machinery."

"But we're talking about uranium," Julie reminded him.

"Well, sure. Uranium is like coal," Ned insisted. "Except that it is much, much more powerful. In fact, one pound of uranium can give as much heat as a hundred and fifty tons of coal."

"Wow!" Julie exclaimed. "One hundred and fifty tons? There are two thousand pounds in a ton, you know."

"I know," Ned said. "Let's see—one hundred and fifty times two thousand pounds—yikes—that's three hundred thousand pounds!"

"You mean that uranium is three hundred thousand times as powerful as coal?" Julie exclaimed.

"Right."

"Well, no wonder it's so valuable," Julie said. "But I'm glad that they don't use it all for atom bombs, anyway."

"So am I," Ned said. "But we're not going

to find enough to fill a small firecracker if we don't get busy."

"You're right," Julie agreed.

"Say!" Ned held the map out so Julie could see. "Did you notice that whoever drew this map doesn't agree at all with those three men we saw out in Wild Horse Canyon?"

"How do you mean, Ned?"

"According to this map, Wild Horse Canyon is a poor place to look for uranium," Ned said. "See, it's not even marked on the map."

"Well, whoever drew that map was only guessing, anyway. Maybe he just forgot to mention Wild Horse Canyon."

"Maybe. But remember we didn't hear anything on the Geiger counter, either, when we were out there," Ned reminded her.

"That's right," Julie replied. "What are you thinking, Ned?"

Ned said, "I just can't help wondering why those men were camped there."

"They said they were uranium prospectors."

"I know. But they didn't act like any uranium prospectors I've ever seen."

73

"Well, it really doesn't matter," Julie said. "I wouldn't care to be friends with them, anyway. They weren't very nice. Besides, we've got other things to do, Ned. Let's forget them."

"O.K.," Ned said, wondering why the three men kept coming back into his mind. "Let's go on." He touched his boot heels gently to Stormy's flanks. The spirited mustang leaped forward and settled into a smooth gallop. Ned held the Geiger counter under one arm to keep it from being jostled around. Julie raced Calico up beside Stormy, and the two horses dodged off through the cactus and sagebrush.

Ned paid slight attention to the direction the horses were taking. He was thinking of the plight of the Rafter B and Box N ranches.

Perhaps it was the scent of water, which the horses could pick up from a great distance, or maybe it was through some unconscious pressure on the reins. Whatever it was—and before either Ned or Julie realized it—the horses had jogged to a trot at the narrow mouth of Wild Horse Canyon.

74

Ned reined to a stop and looked around. He realized that he had had no intention of coming to that place, so why was he there? Had something subconsciously drawn him back to Wild Horse Canyon?

CHAPTER FIVE

"Ned," Julie said, reining Calico up beside him, "I thought we were going to do our prospecting over near Twin Peaks?"

Ned hadn't mentioned anything about going to Twin Peaks, yet it was marked on the newspaper map as a promising location. Also there had been the recent uranium discovery, making the guess a wise one.

"Well," he said, "I suppose that would have been as good a place as any. But I wasn't paying much attention where we were going.

Stormy always seems to head for water. Especially on a hot day like this."

"It isn't far out of our way, at that," Julie said. "As long as we're here, we can ride through the canyon to the far end. Then we can take Apache Gulch out toward Twin Peaks. O.K.?"

"Good idea," Ned agreed.

"Oh, but Ned," Julie said, "what if those three men are still in the canyon? I certainly don't want any more guns pointed at me."

"We have as much right to be in Wild Horse Canyon as they have," Ned insisted. "I —I'm not afraid of them."

Ned didn't say anything about it to Julie, but he had wanted to get another and a closer look at the truck rig, anyway. He had thought of it a lot since the last time he and Julie were in the canyon. And the more he thought, the less it seemed likely that a big van truck like the three men had could simply be a uranium-prospecting outfit.

Besides, Manuel Machado had spoken about some truck driving back and forth at night.

That sort of thing just didn't make sense to Ned.

He even admitted to himself that his curiosity to see the truck up close might have been one of the reasons they now found themselves, for the second time, at the mouth of Wild Horse Canyon.

"Come on," he said. "Nobody is going to bother us."

"I hope you're right," Julie muttered, as she turned her horse to follow Ned.

He picked a course close to the stream. The willows and heavy growth of sage and greasewood offered plenty of good cover for their movements.

"Ned," Julie said finally, "you act as though you're trying to sneak up on that truck."

"Sneak?" Ned said softly. "What makes you think so?"

"Well, if you're not sneaking, why are we going this way?" Julie asked, dodging a willow branch. "And why are you talking so low?"

"No point in making a lot of racket," Ned said, hedging. "And by going this way maybe we can get a better look at the truck."

79

"But why, Ned?"

"I'd just like to, that's all," Ned said evasively.

They threaded their way through the dense undergrowth. Finally, Ned reined Stormy to a stop and held up his hand as a silent warning. Julie eased her pinto up beside him. Her eyes followed the direction of his gaze. The square brown truck was directly ahead. It was half hidden by the low-hanging branches of the willows.

"It's still here, all right," Julie whispered.

"Yeah," Ned said, "but they've moved it." He had noticed right away that the truck was parked deeper in the trees than it had been before. It merely meant that the truck had been used. It recalled again to Ned's mind Manuel Machado's remark about seeing what he thought was a truck shuttling back and forth toward Mesa City at night. If this was the truck, it would account for its being parked in a slightly different place on its return.

"I don't see anyone around," Ned said, after having looked carefully in all directions. "I can see their bedrolls lying there beside the truck. But their campfire is dead cold. Guess they've gone someplace."

"Let's us go, too, Ned," Julie prompted. "I don't want to see them again, or—or have them see us."

"I'd sure like to get a close look at that truck, though," Ned said.

"Oh, no, Ned," Julie protested. "Let's stay away from there. We're supposed to be hunting uranium. Let's do that, Ned."

"We will," Ned said firmly, "in a minute. But first—"

Even as he spoke, he slipped quietly out of his saddle. He hung the Geiger counter over the saddle horn and handed the reins to Julie. "Hold Stormy for me," he said. "I'll be right back."

"Oh, Ned, don't. Please don't."

But Ned already had dropped down on his hands and knees. He crawled carefully through the underbrush toward the truck. Every few seconds he stopped to listen and look around. As there was no sign of life around the truck, he kept moving forward.

81

Having the truck hidden deep in the willows gave him courage. If anyone should come, he would be able to hear them or see them before they saw him. He could make a quick retreat to Julie and the horses.

He stood up cautiously and walked the few remaining yards to the truck. There was still no sign of life, but his heart beat fast with excitement and the fear of being caught.

The boxlike van was even bigger than he had thought from seeing it at a distance. It had extra-large tires. Ned also noticed that the big doors at the back were secured by a heavy padlock. There were no windows whatsoever in the body.

He climbed up onto the running board and looked into the driver's cab. Nothing unusual met his eyes, yet there was something strange about the body of the truck. From several places underneath the floor, water dripped out onto the ground. The drops made a steady splat-splat-splat sound as they hit the ground and immediately sank into the sandy soil. Ned guessed there was a leaky water barrel, or some such thing, inside of the truck.

82

He bent down and caught a few drops of the water in the palm of his hand. It was unusually cold. He put his hand to the flat side of the truck body. It, too, was strangely cold for such a warm day.

Puzzled, and finding nothing else of interest, Ned crouched low and started walking back toward the horses. He took a slightly different route. He had gone but a few yards from the truck, when he suddenly stumbled and fell.

Right in a flat bare space between two clumps of willows the ground had turned soft beneath him. Getting back to his feet, he looked around. The soil was spongy and moist, as though it had been freshly dug. Yes, leaves and twigs had been scattered over the area as though to hide it. Ned was sure that if he hadn't actually stepped upon the ground and been tripped by its softness, he never would have known that it was newly dug.

Why, he wondered, would anyone dig a hole there and then cover it over and carefully camouflage it?

The obvious reason for any hole was to

bury something. Was something buried in that hole? If so, what? And why had the person or persons who dug the hole tried so hard to hide it with leaves and twigs?

Ned didn't have a chance to give much more time to the thought. His ears picked up the sound of horses. He darted a glance out through the willows and saw three horsemen riding leisurely toward the truck. It took no second glance to know they were the same three men he and Julie had happened across the last time they had come out to Wild Horse Canyon.

Half crawling and half running, Ned scurried back through the undergrowth to where Julie waited with the horses.

"Ned, I was afraid—" Julie began.

"Shh-h!" Ned warned quickly. "Be real quiet, Julie."

Ned moved to the heads of the two horses. He put his hands gently over their nostrils. In case either of them should start to whinny at the other horses, he could squeeze slightly and prevent the sound. It was an old Indian and frontiersman's trick.

"Ned, what—what's the matter?" Julie whispered.

"The men are coming back," Ned said softly. "We'd better get out of here. Stay in your saddle, but hand me your reins."

Julie slipped the reins over the pinto's head. Ned picked his route carefully through the willows, until he came to the creek. He walked right into the water. Knee-deep, he led the two horses down the creek away from the direction of the truck. All the while he hoped the other horses hadn't noted their presence, or, if they did, that they wouldn't whinny a greeting.

Luckily, they heard no sounds of pursuit. After he had gone about two hundred yards downstream, Ned led the horses back to the creek bank and handed Julie's reins to her.

"I think we're far enough away," he said, swinging up onto Stormy's back. "Let's beat it."

They rode silently away from the spot. It wasn't until they had once again arrived at the exit from Wild Horse Canyon that Julie reined to a stop and turned to face Ned.

85

"Well, you sure are giving me a wild-goose chase," she accused. "I thought we were going uranium prospecting. And all you've been doing is playing cowboys and Indians."

"Cowboys and Indians?" Ned said.

"Sure. You know what I mean. What kind of a game was that you were playing by sneaking up on an empty truck?"

"It was no game, Julie," Ned defended himself. "And just what makes you think the truck was empty?"

"Even if it wasn't empty, who cares what's inside of it?" Julie asked.

"Maybe we'd both care if we knew," Ned argued. "I've got an idea that something mighty funny is going on. And that truck is part of it."

"All right," Julie said sharply. "There's something funny. You tell me what it is."

Ned bit down on his lower lip. Actually, he didn't have any real idea. He didn't even know why he felt the way he did. Even less, he had no way of knowing how it might all tie in with him, or with Julie, or with their plans for hunting uranium.

He realized suddenly that he might not have been playing fair with Julie. Perhaps she was right. Perhaps he had been playing cowboys and Indians, when he should have stuck to what they had started out to do. After all, it was very important to both of them that they make their uranium discovery just as quickly as possible. The more he thought of it, the more he had become convinced that the discovery of uranium was the one thing that could save the Rafter B and the Box N ranches. The cattle were simply nowhere to be found.

"I'm sorry, Julie," he apologized. "Guess I've been trying to play a little detective or something, at that." He patted the Geiger counter, which he had removed from the saddle horn, and hung it back over his shoulder. "Let's go find our uranium."

"Now you're talking," Julie said happily. "Let's not worry any more about those three men, or their truck, or what they are doing. Anyway, it's really none of our business."

Ned didn't answer. There was no point in arguing further with Julie.

But, try as he would, Ned couldn't shake off the thought of the men with the truck. Nor could he think of any logical reason for the carefully filled and hidden hole that had tripped him up. The thought kept crowding back that the hole, the truck, and the men all had some part in the plight of the Box N and the Rafter B.

Maybe, even, it was a very big part.

CHAPTER SIX

Twice during the following week Ned and Julie took the Geiger counter and rode out to sections marked on the newspaper map as likely spots to find uranium-bearing ore. During those two days they both came to realize that hunting for uranium was one thing—finding it, quite another. A couple of times they located outcroppings of rock which caused the clicking in the Geiger counter to speed up a little. They counted the number of clicks per minute. Then they checked it against the printed instructions pasted on the back of the counter. Both times they found the ore was

"Unless it is pretty rich ore it isn't worth digging."

quite a bit under what was called commercial grade.

"Unless it is pretty rich ore," Ned explained, "it isn't worth digging and having to haul to a mill."

"I guess I know what you mean," Julie said. "It's like shipping a skinny steer to market. If there's not enough meat to pay the freight cost, there's no sense in shipping it. Right?"

"Right. And you can't make any money that way, either," Ned added. "To tell you the truth, Julie, we don't seem to be getting anywhere with our uranium prospecting. I'm beginning to see why Mr. Medford went back home and gave his Geiger counter to us. Discovering uranium is a lot harder than it may sound."

"But we mustn't give up, Ned," Julie said anxiously. "We can't be quitters."

There was an urgency in her voice that verged upon desperation.

"We won't give up, Julie," Ned promised. "Not yet, anyway. But I'm afraid I can't go prospecting tomorrow. Dad said this morning that there were some chores he wanted me to do. He has to go in to Mesa City for a couple of days."

"That's funny," Julie said. "My father's going to Mesa City, too. I wonder if they're going together?"

"Probably," Ned said. He wondered why his father hadn't mentioned about Mr. Nelson going, also. Was there any reason to be mysterious about the trip?

Ned dismissed the thought from his mind. If his father had wanted him to know all the details, he would have told him. "If you want to, Julie," he said, "you can take the Geiger counter and go prospecting tomorrow. You don't need me."

"Oh, I wouldn't want to go without you, Ned," Julie said. "Besides, I don't think I could work the thing. It sure looks complicated—all those dials and switches and earphones and things."

"It's easy to work," Ned assured her. "Once you switch it on, you just listen to the clicks in the earphones. Or you watch that needle on the dial. If the needle jumps way over to the right, and the clicks practically hum in your

92

ears—well, probably we wouldn't have to worry about the ranches or the missing cattle any more. We'd have uranium. And, boy, that's a lot more valuable than beef."

"But I bet it's not nearly as much fun to raise," Julie said.

"Maybe," Ned admitted.

"Anyway," Julie said, "I still think I'll wait until we can go together. Maybe in a day or two, huh?"

"I'll do my best," Ned promised. "I'll work hard on my chores."

So it was that on the following day Ned was chopping weeds around the horse barn at the Rafter B when he saw a small figure hurrying across the field toward him. Ned paused in his hoeing and mopped at his sweaty forehead, as he watched the person approach. Then he saw it was Manuel Machado. He figured quickly that the Mexican boy wanted to drive his sheep in for some water. It was a hot day. Once in a while a shepherd let his flock graze too far from water. Then he had to beg or buy some from the cattle ranchers. The ranchers didn't like the idea, but there was not one of them who would stand by and let any animal—even sheep—suffer from thirst.

As soon as he got inside of the log gate, Manuel spied Ned.

"Hello, Ned," he called, changing his direction toward the barn. "Got a minute?"

"Just about," Ned said curtly. "I've got all of these weeds to chop."

"Phew!" Manuel said, stepping into the shade beside the barn and wiping his face with a blue bandanna. "Sure is hot. O.K. if I go over to the windmill and get a drink?"

"You or your sheep?" Ned asked suspiciously

"Just me," Manuel said, appearing a little hurt by the question. "I take care of my sheep, Ned. I have never gone to any cattle rancher to beg for water." He said it proudly, as though he wanted Ned to know that he could stand on his own two feet. "Anyway, I didn't come to see you about a drink—for me or my sheep. I just thought you might be interested to know that I saw some of your cattle this morning."

94

"You did?" Ned said, perking up quickly. "Where, Manuel?"

The Mexican boy seemed in no big rush. He ran his tongue around his dry lips. "Phew! Sure am thirsty," he said.

"You better not be telling me a fib," Ned challenged. "About the cattle, I mean. Where did you see them?" But Ned knew it was useless to try rushing the information out of Manuel. It just wasn't the Mexican boy's way to be hurried.

Manuel walked over to the windmill tank. Ned followed. He fidgeted while the Mexican herder paused politely beside the water overflow pipe at the top of the tank.

"Help yourself," Ned invited. "Drink all you want. But tell me, where did you see some Rafter B cattle?"

"No big hurry, Ned," Manuel said. He cupped his hands skillfully and filled them under the trickle of cool water. "They found a patch of grass. They'll stay there all right."

"Where? How many?" Ned demanded.

Manuel drank his fill. Then he straightened up, wiped his lips with his bandanna, and, finally, turned to answer Ned's urgent questions.

"Well," he said, "all told there were eight head."

"All told? What do you mean?"

"Three head carried the Box N brand," Manuel said.

"Good," Ned said, thinking how pleased Julie would be. It was common on the open range for cattle from different ranches to be found grazing together. It was especially common for Rafter B and Box N cattle to be mixed together, because the ranches joined each other. "And were the other five head all Rafter B?"

"Yep," Manuel answered.

"Boy," Ned said, "Dad sure will be glad to find even that many. So will Mr. Nelson. Where are they, Manuel?"

"They're over between Wild Horse Canyon and Twin Peaks," the Mexican boy said. "I was working my flock that way when I spotted them. You know where Hidden Canyon is?"

"Just about," Ned said. "I've only been out there once."

Hidden Canyon was little more than a dead-end gulch, not far from Wild Horse Canyon. People seldom went there. It was a barren canyon, without water and with very little grass. In fact, years ago the ranchers had strung a couple of strands of barbed wire across the narrow mouth of Hidden Canyon to keep cattle from wandering inside and not being able to find their way out again. Before the wire had been strung, quite a few cattle had been lost in the canyon.

"I'll show you where they are if you want me to," Manuel volunteered.

"Swell," Ned said. "My dad's in town, but I'll go tell my mother. If we go now, I should be able to drive them back here to the ranch by nightfall."

"Then you'd better hurry," the Mexican youth said. "It's a pretty good ride from here."

When Ned returned from telling his mother the good news, he roped and saddled Stormy.

97

"Why don't you take your Geiger counter with you, Ned?" Manuel suggested. "There are a lot of rocks around Hidden Canyon. Can't tell, you might just run across some uranium." The young sheepherder smiled shyly and added, "I've been reading about uranium hunting, too. Someday maybe I'll get me a Geiger counter."

"I haven't had much luck with mine," Ned said.

"Well, a fellow has to keep trying," Manuel said.

"Guess so," Ned admitted. "Besides, like you say, I might kill two birds with one stone, huh?" He hurried back to the ranch house and returned with the Geiger counter.

"Come on," he invited, pulling his left boot out of the stirrup. "Swing up here. You can ride behind me."

Smiling his appreciation, the Mexican boy vaulted lightly up and settled himself behind the saddle cantle. "I can carry the Geiger counter," he offered. "Guess you're not supposed to bang them around much, huh?"

"That's right," Ned said, handing the black

98

box back to the Mexican youth. "I think I'll swing by the Box N and tell Julie," he announced, as they started away from the ranch buildings. "She sure will be glad to hear about the Box N cattle, even if there are only three of them."

"Three steers make a lot of sheep," Manuel said by way of stressing the importance of even so few head.

"Guess you're right there," Ned agreed. He slacked off on the reins. Stormy set out at a fast canter. Manuel rode skillfully behind Ned.

A little later Julie rushed out of the ranch house as Ned reined Stormy to a stop near the front. Quickly, he told her about the cattle.

"Oh, that's wonderful!" Julie exclaimed. "I'll go with you."

"Maybe it would be better if a grownup went," Ned suggested. "Your father, maybe." He was thinking of how much quicker and easier it might be to round up the cattle and get them headed back to the ranches if Mr. Nelson were along to help.

"Ned, you sure do forget quick," Julie

scolded. "Daddy went to Mesa City with your father this morning. Won't be back until late tomorrow."

Ned hadn't been out of bed when his father left for Mesa City early that morning, and he had forgotten that Mr. Nelson was going also.

"Oh, that's right," he said. "Well, I hope they get their shopping done and get back soon. They'll sure be glad to—"

"Shopping?" Julie interrupted. "They didn't go shopping. They went to see Mr. Leland at the bank." She glanced at Manuel. "I guess you know what about, Ned," she added meaningfully.

Ned nodded slowly. Although his father wasn't one to talk money matters much, it seemed quite certain now that the Rafter B was in as bad financial shape as the Box N.

It was a thought that had occurred to Ned before. But he had always managed to crowd it from his mind. Besides, he didn't know much about bank loans and such things as that. He hadn't really cared, for that matter.

But he cared now—cared a whole lot.

After checking with her mother, Julie returned and went for Calico. Manuel handed Ned the Geiger counter and quickly slipped down from behind the saddle. He helped Julie rig the pinto for riding. Then the young sheepherder swung up behind Ned again.

"Whillikers!" Ned exclaimed after they had ridden quite a distance from the ranch. "You really had some walk to the Rafter B, leaving your sheep and everything."

"I didn't mind," Manuel said. "I know the sheep are safe with Chico."

But Ned was thinking that not many people would have gone to all that trouble, especially for someone who had never been very friendly. Ned certainly was glad he hadn't left Manuel standing back at the Rafter B as he almost had done.

All three young people jerked their heads toward the sound of sudden loud barking.

"That's Chico," Manuel said. "The sheep must be just over that rise."

"Hold on!" Ned said quickly. "Sounds like he's having trouble."

"It certainly does," Julie said.

"Hold on tight, Manuel," Ned said. He

spurred Stormy into a gallop. The ground flew past beneath them. When they reached the top of the rise, Ned reined Stormy to a stop. The three of them sat and looked with amusement at the scene below.

Barking and nipping at their flying heels, the sheepdog was trying desperately to chase a dozen or so sheep back into the main flock. Ned had never seen a dog working so hard.

Laughing, Manuel slipped the strap of the Geiger counter off his shoulder and handed the instrument to Ned. "Think I better leave you now," he said. "Chico's a good dog. But see how the sheep try to fool him when he's alone. I'll give him a hand."

"We'll help you," Julie offered.

"Thanks, but I won't have any trouble," the Mexican boy said. Then he pointed ahead. "Oh, yeah, I almost forgot. Your cattle are just beyond that knoll over there."

"Good," Ned said. "We'll find them all right." He reined Stormy along the edge of the browsing flock. Strangely, he felt an absence of the usual resentment at the sight of the sheep. "Manuel," he said, as the boy prepared to slide down to the ground, "thanks a lot for coming to tell us about the cattle."

"I hope someday we can do you a favor," Julie added.

"It was nothing, my friends," the young sheepherder said, dropping to the ground. "Ouch!"

"What's the matter?" Ned asked quickly. "Hurt yourself?"

"Naw. I should have looked where I was lighting," Manuel said. "Just twisted my ankle a little in that tire rut. Doesn't hurt any now, though," he added as he shook his leg.

For the first time Ned noticed the tire ruts Manuel spoke of. He saw that they were broad and sank rather deeply into the sandy soil.

"Those look as though they were made by the same truck we saw in Wild Horse Canyon the other day," he said musingly. "Manuel, have you seen any more trucks running at night lately?"

"A couple of times since I saw you and Julie last," the young herder said. "Well, one night I saw the lights. The other night I only heard the motor. I guess it might have been the same truck. I don't know for sure, though, Ned. I've never really had a good look at it —not even the night it ran down some of my sheep. Besides, it never seems to follow any regular road."

"Well, a guy doesn't need to worry much about roads out here," Ned said. "It's fairly flat and smooth. With a little dodging he can drive almost anyplace without roads."

"Anyway," Julie interrupted, "let's talk about trucks some other time. We'd better round up those cattle and start heading back before it gets dark."

"Yeah, you're right," Ned admitted. But he kept wondering about that mysterious truck.

"Good luck," Manuel called as they started off. "If I see any more cattle before I get back to Mesa City with the flock, I'll let you know somehow."

"Swell," Ned called back over his shoulder. "Thanks, Manuel. Thanks a lot."

"If we don't see you sooner," Julie added, "we'll see you when school starts again."

"Sure thing," the Mexican boy replied. "Just ride straight ahead. It's not far."

"He's a nice fellow, isn't he?" Julie said to Ned as they rode away.

"Yeah," Ned admitted. "If he just wasn't a sheepman."

They rode on around the knoll Manuel had pointed out. Ned turned slowly in his saddle, looking all around, a puzzled expression on his face.

"According to Manuel, we should be seeing them by now," he said.

"Maybe they wandered into some gully," Julie suggested.

Ned reined Stormy to a halt. He shaded his eyes with his hand and peered ahead toward the greenish-gray patch near the edge of a low, flat mesa.

"That must be the grass Manuel talked about," he said. "It looks like a good patch. If I know cattle, they wouldn't be quick to wander away from it. Come on. Let's go have a close look."

"Race you to it," Julie suggested quickly.

"Yee-ee-up!" Ned yelled. Stormy leaped forward in a ground-eating gallop.

"Hii-ee-yah!" Julie's shrill cry echoed

through the sagebrush, as the two horses raced across the gently rolling ground.

For a few yards Julie's Calico pulled up beside Stormy. The thunder of galloping hoofs was pleasant music to Ned's ears.

"Go, Stormy," he coaxed. "Go!"

The black mustang stretched out for all he was worth. Even so, he had barely pulled away from Julie's pinto by the time they reached the patch of grass.

Ned reined Stormy in. "Phew-w!" he said breathlessly. "Calico and Stormy are a good pair. Good race, huh?"

"We'll beat you next time," Julie said, laughing.

But suddenly she forgot the race. Standing in her stirrups, she looked around carefully in every direction. "Say, I wonder if Manuel gave us a bad lead," she said. "I sure don't see any cattle around here."

"They've been here all right," Ned said, slipping to the ground. "See their tracks around? Fresh tracks, too."

"But where could they have gone?" Julie

asked. "They wouldn't have wandered far away in such a short time."

"Unless something scared them, or drove them off," Ned said tensely. He dropped to one knee and began inspecting the ground.

"But what could have frightened them, Ned?" Julie asked. "Way out here. Even a snake wouldn't make them move far."

"It wasn't a snake," Ned said, "unless it was a two-legged snake."

"What do you mean by that?" Julie said in alarm.

Ned got back to his feet. Julie saw that his face had turned pale. "Julie," he said, "there are horse tracks mixed in here with the cattle tracks. And there aren't any horses coming out here unless they have riders on them. I think someone has run off our cattle."

"But—but that's crazy, Ned," Julie insisted. "Who would do a thing like that?"

Ned took a deep breath and looked at her.

"Rustlers," he said firmly. "That's who!"

CHAPTER SEVEN

Saying it was one thing. Actually believing that the cattle had been stolen by rustlers was quite another. After all, this wasn't the old frontier West; this was the new, modern West. This was the West that had super highways, frozen foods, soapless detergents, and fantastic arrays of plastic items. Of course, the ranchers still rode horses and raised cattle, but most of them also had a jeep or some kind of an automobile parked in the garage or beside the corral.

There just didn't seem to be any place to

fit in the old time-worn word, "rustling." There seemed to be even less chance for such a thing actually to happen. Yet Ned had read plenty of Western history and had listened to some of the old-timers talk. And right now, with the evidence there before him, rustling seemed the only logical explanation for the missing steers.

Julie didn't seem to agree with his idea. "Ned, you're being really old-fashioned," she accused. "How in the world could anyone actually rustle cattle these days? Maybe the ranches aren't right side by side like the houses are in the city, but even as far apart as they are, do you think anyone could drive cattle out of this area without being seen?"

"Well, it wouldn't be easy," Ned admitted. "But someone must be doing it. How else can you figure it? We should have thought of it before."

"What if someone did rustle them," Julie said by way of argument. "Where could they take them?"

"Mesa City, of course."

"But everyone at the packing house in Mesa City knows our brands. They would never accept the cattle without your father or mine being there to make the sale. They've been doing it that way for years."

"That's true," Ned agreed, "but there are a lot of restaurants and eating places in Mesa City. They must use a lot of beef."

"Well, for goodness sakes, Ned," Julie said, "you don't go around rustling cattle and then drive them up to a restaurant door. That's really a silly idea."

Ned had to admit that it sounded rather foolish. He felt the warm blood rush into his cheeks. Still, he was convinced in his own mind that the mixture of horse and cattle tracks scattered on the ground around him meant rustlers.

"Let's follow the tracks," he said. "We'll see." He started circling the patch of grass. He found where the tracks left the grazing area.

"Here they are," he called, pointing. "They go up that bluff and—"

111

"And right across the rimrock, probably," Julie finished. "We sure can't track anything across that solid rock, Ned."

Ned knew Julie was right. It was practically impossible to track anything across the rimrock. At the same time, it was unlikely the cattle would have gone that way unless they were driven. The rocks bruised and cut their hoofs. Cattle avoided the hard, rocky ground whenever possible.

Ned was at a loss to know just what to do. If only his father were there, or Mr. Nelson. Why, of all times, did they both have to be in Mesa City? Ned felt that the matter of the missing cattle couldn't wait until their return. Something had to be done right away. This was the first time in months that there had been any real clue to go on. He simply had to follow it up.

"Ned, I have an idea," Julie called. "It isn't far over to Wild Horse Canyon. Let's go over and ask those uranium prospectors if they have seen the cattle, or anyone with them."

"You mean let's go see if they have our cattle!" Ned suggested.

"I don't mean that at all," Julie said, riding up and handing Stormy's reins to Ned. "Why do you say that? Maybe they acted a little strange the first time we met them. But I guess if someone came around while we were hunting uranium we might not act so friendly, either."

"I sure wouldn't act like they did," Ned said.

Yet Ned didn't feel there was much point of going into the reasons that made him suspicious of the three strangers. After all, he didn't really have anything solid to go by. He knew so little about uranium prospecting that he certainly had no way of proving whether the men were prospectors or not.

"They can't do any more than send us away," Julie insisted. "Only we'll ride straight into their camp, and not do any snooping. We'll just ask them if they've seen the cattle. We have to do something, Ned. Or else we never will get our cattle back."

"I—I guess you're right, Julie," Ned said. He was still bending down looking at the mixture of horse and cattle tracks that angled up the low bluff and disappeared when they reached the rimrock. "You know something?" he went on. "One of the horses has a shoe missing from its left hind hoof."

"How do you know that?"

"Easy. Just look at the tracks."

"Well, you have sharp eyes," Julie said, "but I don't see how finding that a horse has a missing shoe is very important to us."

Ned didn't answer. He slung the strap of the Geiger counter back over his shoulder and swung up into the saddle.

They rode off in the direction of Wild Horse Canyon. Although Ned's mind was mainly on the missing cattle, he stopped once and dismounted near a rock slide at the foot of a crumbling hill.

"Let's take a reading while we're here," he said. He switched on the Geiger counter. Walking through the jumble of rocks, he held the sensitive probe down close to them. Only once did the clicking increase enough to cause him to pause. Then he moved on. "Doesn't click fast enough to be worth while," he explained to Julie, who still sat astride Calico. "But there's some uranium around here, all right. One of these times we'll hit a real hot spot."

"I sure hope so," Julie said. "But, Ned, the sun is almost down. We'd better get moving, hadn't we?"

Ned nodded and remounted. As they approached Wild Horse Canyon, he automatically picked his course through a series of rain-washed gullies.

"Ned," Julie said after a few minutes, "why do we stay in the gullies? It's easier to ride on the mesa, and—well, you always act as though you are trying to sneak up on those men."

Ned realized that it was exactly what he had been doing, although he had not thought of it that way.

"I think we should ride straight in, Ned," Julie said. "After all, there is no reason to sneak up. The men won't like it one bit."

Julie was right. Ned reined Stormy out of

115

the gully and onto the mesa. Within a few minutes they reached the edge of the mesa that overlooked Wild Horse Canyon. They rode down the slanting bluff and headed for the large clump of willows that marked the strangers' camp site. Darkness was coming on fast as the sun dropped below the western hills.

"Ned," Julie said when they were still a half mile from the camp site, "I don't see the truck."

Ned peered through the dusk. "It's gone, all right," he confirmed.

"Well, I guess that's that," Julie said. "Probably they didn't find any uranium and moved on to some other place."

"Could be," Ned said. "Anyway, I guess we're too late."

"There's nothing more we can do," Julie said, pulling Calico to a stop. "And we'd better head on home. It'll be after dark when we get there. I don't want to worry my mother."

"O.K.," Ned agreed. Although he had a desire to go on to the camp site and have a

116

look around, he didn't relish the idea of riding home in darkness, either.

Julie already had reined Calico toward home. Ned was starting to follow, when Stormy flicked his ears forward and whinnied.

"Hold it, Julie," Ned called quickly. "There's something over behind that rock outcropping."

The proof was fast coming. Ned had no more than spoken the words than a return whinny floated toward them from the direction of the high rocks.

"A horse," Julie said. "Ned, that's right where we heard that horse nicker the first day we were out here."

"Yeah," Ned said, "and those men tried to make us believe it was a wild burro or something. Come on. Let's have a look."

"Oh, Ned," Julie protested, "do you think we should?"

"Nothing wrong with looking at a horse," Ned insisted. "Might even be trapped or hurt or something."

With Julie following close behind, he guided Stormy around the rocks. They found

117

not one but three horses staked out in an oval-shaped clearing which nature had carved out of the surrounding rocks. There were wadded chunks of baling wire lying around. Over to one side were several unopened bales of hay. The horses had been munching on parts of an opened bale. Now they stood, ears cocked forward, watching the newcomers approach.

"Someone just fed them not long ago," Ned said in a low voice. "They haven't even had time to finish their hay."

"There are their saddles and bridles," Julie added, pointing to the collection of riding gear on a nearby flat rock.

Ned dismounted and walked slowly up to the horses. Gently, he laid his hand against the side of one bay gelding. "They're not even cooled off," he said over his shoulder. "They've been ridden hard within the past hour or so."

"But who owns them?" Julie wondered.

"Who else but those three men with the truck," Ned said.

"But they're not even here any more, Ned,"

118

Julie reminded him. "They wouldn't drive their truck away and leave their horses."

"Not for long, anyway," Ned agreed. "Something sure is fishy, Julie."

"There you go again," Julie scolded. "More mysteries. Ned, maybe the men have taken the truck to some new location, and will come back for their horses."

"Why didn't they save the trouble and lead the horses from the back of the truck?" Ned asked. "Why leave them here? And if they are uranium prospectors, why the horses in the first place?"

"You're not talking sense now, Ned," Julie said. "We're uranium prospectors, and we have horses, don't we? And horses can go a lot of places a truck can't."

Ned really didn't have any answer to that. As a matter of fact, he was hardly listening to Julie, for while she was talking, another thought had come into his mind. It was a very important thought.

Talking soothingly to the bay horse, he moved his hand gently down its left hind leg. He lifted the hoof, looked, then let it down again. He moved next to the silver-gray standing nearby. He repeated the action, while Julie watched, puzzled.

Suddenly Ned straightened up. Already it had grown too dark for Julie to see his lips move, but Ned's words were startlingly crisp and clear.

"Julie," he exclaimed, "this gray—his—his left hind shoe is missing!"

CHAPTER EIGHT

The long silence which followed Ned's announcement was broken by Julie's tense whisper. "Ned, let's get out of here! If they should come back—"

"You're right," Ned agreed quickly. Discovering the horse with the missing shoe had erased all doubt from Ned's mind about the men being responsible for the cattles' disappearance.

"We'd better ride to Mesa City and get the sheriff," he said, moving toward Stormy.

"Mesa City?" Julie said. "Ned, Mesa City

must be twenty miles from here! We'll be lucky to find our way back home in the dark."

"But what if those men get away?" Ned asked.

"They're not going to leave their horses and saddles here," Julie reminded him. "They've got to come back. But there's no way to know when. Ned, let's hurry home. In the morning my mother could drive us to town in the pickup truck. Maybe even tonight. She'll know where to find our fathers. We'll get Sheriff Kincaid, too. He'll know just what to do."

Ned's first impulse was to argue. He wanted to do something immediately. The men couldn't be caught any too soon, and put in jail. Yet he had to admit it would be somewhat foolish to try riding to Mesa City in the dark over unfamiliar ground.

"All right, Julie," he agreed. "We'll do as you say. Guess we'd make a lot faster time in the pickup, anyway."

"Sure," Julie said. "Come on."

Ned swung up into the saddle. "Better

stick close together, Julie," he said. "It sure is getting dark. We've got to be careful."

They had ridden for a few minutes when Ned reined Stormy to a halt. Julie nearly toppled from her saddle when Calico stopped to keep from bumping into Ned's mustang.

"Hey, what's the idea?" Julie protested.

"Look," Ned said. "What's that glow in the sky over there?"

"Over where?"

"Look where I'm pointing."

"How can I see where you're pointing in this darkness?" Julie said. She urged Calico up closer beside Ned's horse until she saw the outline of Ned's outstretched arm.

"See it?" Ned asked again.

"Yes, I see it, Ned. Must be the glow from the moon down over the horizon."

"The moon comes up in the east," Ned said, "and that's due south."

"You're right," Julie admitted. "But what do you suppose it is, then? A campfire?"

"It might be," Ned said.

"Well, anyway, it's not our worry," Julie said. "Let's keep going home."

But Ned was not ready to dismiss the glow that easily. It certainly was unusual that there would be any kind of a light way out there miles from any place.

"It looks like it's over near Hidden Canyon," he said in growing excitement. "That's not far from here."

"Now, Ned, I hope you're not figuring to—"

But Ned had already made up his mind. "It'll just take a few minutes," he said. "It's not going to get any darker, anyway. And, if it's campers, we won't even disturb them. I promise."

"And if it isn't campers?" Julie asked. "What then, Ned?"

It was apparent to Ned that Julie was thinking the same thing that had been filling his mind. That glow might be from the lights of the missing truck. Yet, it didn't seem to be moving. Why would the truck—if that's what it was—be parked over toward Hidden Canyon at that time of night with its lights blazing?

"Come on," Ned said, "I'm going to have a look."

Using the dim glow in the sky as a guide, the two rode carefully out of Wild Horse Canyon and across the rocky mesa. Ned tried hard to remember the way to Hidden Canyon. It had been a long time since he had ridden there. After the narrow mouth of the canyon had been fenced off, the ranchers had little occasion ever to go there. Stormy kept wanting to turn toward home, but Ned held a firm rein on him, guiding the mustang toward the glow in the sky.

As they approached the upper edge of the narrow canyon, the light grew steadily brighter. Ned reined Stormy in.

"Let's leave the horses here, Julie," he said softly. "We—we can crawl to the edge of the canyon and look down."

"Oh, Ned," Julie protested, "do you think we should go snooping?"

"Why not?" Ned said. "If it's just some campers, it won't matter. They won't even see us. If it isn't—well, come on. Or stay, if you want."

"I'll go," Julie said.

They tied their horses to a clump of sage. Ned hung the Geiger counter over the horn of Stormy's saddle. They moved cautiously toward the edge of the bluff that overlooked Hidden Canyon. When they were a few yards from the drop-off, Ned got down on his hands and knees and crawled forward. Julie followed close behind him.

Reaching the edge of the bluff, Ned looked down. The sight that met his eyes caused him to suck in his breath sharply. Almost directly below them, at the foot of the steeply slanting bluff, three men worked feverishly in the glare of the truck head lamps.

In a glance Ned saw that they were the same men who had been in Wild Horse Canyon that first day he and Julie had gone uranium prospecting. There was the burly Brock, the tall, blond Slim, and the chubby, balding Tabor.

"What—what are they doing, Ned?" Julie whispered.

At first Ned was too amazed at the sight to answer. It was quite obvious what the men

126

were preparing to do. Near the front of the truck they had built a tall rack, or scaffold, of logs. It came to a peak like the poles of an Indian tepee. The men had rigged a rope and pulley where the upper tips came together. At the moment, all three of them were standing and inspecting it.

Beyond, but still within reach of the truck headlights, several head of cattle were grouped against the canyon wall.

"Should be plenty strong," Brock's familiar voice floated up to the young pair. He shook the rack to test its firmness. "All right, let's get busy."

The three men picked up coils of rope and turned toward the dead end of the canyon.

"The—the cattle!" Julie whispered, seeing them for the first time. Although they couldn't make out the brands in the dim light, Ned had no doubt they were the missing Rafter B and Box N cattle which Manuel Machado had seen.

"Ned," Julie whispered," wh-what are they doing with those steers?"

"Nothing yet, Julie," Ned spoke softly in

her ear. "But I think they're getting ready to butcher them."

"Butcher them?"

"Shh-h!" he cautioned. "That truck—it's a refrigerator truck." He knew now the reason for the cold water dripping out from beneath the truck the day he had inspected it in Wild Horse Canyon. The water was from melting ice, which the men no doubt picked up during their trips to Mesa City. "They are going to butcher our cattle right here on the spot. They've already dug the hole for burying the hides and stuff. After they butcher, they'll haul the beef right on in to Mesa City."

It was all very clear to him now. It also explained the carefully filled-in and camouflaged hole he had stumbled over that day in Wild Horse Canyon.

These were modern-day rustlers. They used a refrigerator truck to deliver quartered and brandless beef, rather than the more risky and old-fashioned method of trying to sell branded live steers.

"No, Ned," Julie protested. "I'm scared. What if they see us up here? Let's go! Now!"

As Julie started to push back from the edge of the bluff, the ground suddenly gave way beneath her.

"Eee-yow!" Julie's shrill and startled screech filled the night.

Ned tried to grab her as she slipped over the edge. He got hold of a foot and held on. But the added weight caused more of the ground to give way. He clutched for a clump of grass, but it pulled free.

Suddenly he and Julie began sliding and tumbling down the steeply slanting bluff. There was nothing to grab, no way to stop. One of Julie's flailing elbows crashed painfully into Ned's cheek. As he somersaulted, his shoulder banged against a rock. Julie uttered a series of painful sobs, as they rolled and tumbled to the bottom of the bluff.

Then the startled shouts of the men filled the night.

"Ouch, Ned, you're on my arm!" Julie cried, as they came to a stop.

Ned rolled over carefully and jumped to his feet. "You all right?" he asked quickly.

"I—I think so," Julie said, "but—"

"Then get up. We've got to make a run for it!"

"Then get up. We've got to make a run for it, Julie!" Ned's words were urgent, as he heard footsteps hurrying toward them.

Julie scrambled up. Ned grabbed her hand, pulling her along after him in the darkness. He wasn't at all sure which direction to take, but he kept running and slipping. The loose dirt and rocks beneath his boots gave way and he fell again, losing his hold on Julie's hand. As he struggled back up, rough hands grabbed him. He heard Julie's frightened squeal, and knew that she too was captured.

They were half carried and half dragged to the front of the truck. There, in the glare from the head lamps, they looked up into the familiar and angry faces of their captors.

"Well," the man named Brock said, "if it ain't our young friends again." There was no sign of amusement or friendship on his face.

"I told you, Brock," Slim said. "We should have left while the going was good. I figured these nosy kids would come snooping around again sometime and foul up the works."

"Slim's right," Tabor said. "Maybe they're not alone, and—"

131

"They're alone or we'd be hearin' from any others by now," Brock said. "Slim, climb up that bluff and see if you can find their horses up top. Be on the lookout, though, just in case there is anyone else around. How about it, kids, you alone?"

Ned didn't answer. He watched the tall thin man climbing carefully up the same part of the bluff that he and Julie had tumbled down.

"You—you've been stealing our cattle!" Julie accused the men. "You're not uranium prospectors at all!"

"Now, now, ain't you the smart young one," Tabor said. "And why would we have this if we ain't uranium hunters?" He reached into the front window of the truck and brought out a small square box.

"It—it's a Geiger counter, all right, isn't it, Ned?" Julie asked.

"Sure," Ned said, "but that doesn't mean a thing. They might carry a counter just in case some rancher happened by and wondered what they were doing out here. Anyone can buy a Geiger counter. Even rent one. That looks like a cheap one, too. Bet they don't even know how to work it."

"That kid's too smart for us, Brock," Tabor said. "Bet he knows everything that's going on."

"Don't doubt it," Brock said. "Matter of fact, he's too smart for his own good. O.K., youngster. So we ain't uranium hunters. So what are you goin' to do about it?"

"I'm going to tell my father," Julie said hotly.

Tabor laughed. "And just how do you figure to do that, young one? You're not going to tell anybody anything."

Brock picked up a coil of rope he had dropped in the dirt when Ned and Julie had tumbled down the bluff. He tossed it over to Tabor. "Better tie them up," he said. "I'll figure what we'll do next."

"Let's get out of here," Tabor said quickly. "The jig's up. At least around here."

Slim came back into the wedge of light from the truck's head lamps. He was riding Stormy and leading Calico. "Mighty fine horses these kids have," he commented. "Lot better than ours. Maybe we should trade."

"You'd better not," Ned spoke up quickly.

"Any signs of anyone else up there, Slim?" Tabor asked.

"Nope," Slim said. "Reckon these kids were just nosing around by themselves. Well, what now, boss?" He turned to Brock.

"Guess Tabor's right," the ringleader said. "We better forget that last bunch of cattle and head out of here. Can't tell when someone might be following these kids out. Go pick up the horses with the truck. We've had good enough pickin's around here, anyway. Won't hurt us to forget those last few steers."

The fat man, Tabor, had begun tying Julie's and Ned's hands behind them. At first Ned struggled. But Tabor was too strong for him. Julie tried to yell, only to have Tabor stuff a gag in her mouth and tie it tight.

"Now, if you're smart, kid, you won't yell and get gagged, too," he said to Ned.

After the two young people were securely bound, Slim turned to the leader. "You can't just leave them out here, Brock. I don't figure to have any part of doing harm to a couple kids."

Brock said, "There won't nothin' happen to 'em if they behave. I got that all figured. But we can't just turn them loose, either. We need time to get out of this part of the country —far out of it."

"That's right," Tabor spoke up. "These punk kids had no business nosing around here. They got to take their medicine."

"When Sheriff Kincaid catches you," Ned said, "you—you'll be in jail in a hurry."

"Sure, sure," Brock replied, laughing. "But he ain't goin' to catch us. No one else, either. First thing everyone's goin' to do is start lookin' for you. By the time they find you, we'll be hundreds of miles away from here. O.K., Slim, let's start packin'. Tabor, turn the truck around."

Ned and Julie watched as the three men prepared to leave. Ned's idea about the refrigerated truck was confirmed when Slim climbed inside and started pushing large cakes of ice out onto the ground. "We won't need that stuff," he said, "and it will make more room for the horses."

Soon the truck was ready to leave.

"How about it, Brock?" Slim suggested. "Let's take these horses. They're beauties."

"Nope," Brock said. "I've got use for those horses."

He walked over to where Ned and Julie lay on the ground, tied hand and foot. "All right, kids, here's how it is. You got yourselves into this by snoopin' around. You might get a little hungry before anyone finds you, but that should be about all. If you can keep your mouth shut now, girlie, I'll take off the gag. O.K.?"

Julie nodded her head vigorously. Brock leaned down and untied the gag.

"You—you can't leave us here!" Ned protested. "Not tied up!"

"No one ever comes here to Hidden Canyon any more," Julie said. "We—we'll starve before—"

"They'll come out here when they know that you're lost," Brock assured her. "But it

136

may take a little while. That's the idea, and you won't starve. Everyone will be busy lookin' for you, and it'll give us lots of time to get plenty far away."

Ned tried to protest again, but his mouth was suddenly too dry to talk. Julie was right. People seldom came to Hidden Canyon any more. And a person couldn't last long lying out in the sun, tied hand and foot.

"We'll send your horses high-tailin' it home," Brock explained. "Don't worry, there'll be plenty of search parties out after you as soon as the horses arrive at the ranches with empty saddles. With no gags, you can start shoutin' if you hear anyone around. How's that? Good enough deal?"

"It certainly is not," Julie protested. "And you—you better not try it!"

"It's the best we can do," Brock said firmly. "Ready, Slim?"

"All set."

"You too, Tabor?"

"Let's get going, boss," the heavy man said. He climbed into the truck cab.

Brock lifted the Geiger counter from where it hung over Stormy's saddle horn.

"Here," he said, laying the instrument on the ground. "I'll leave you kids your counter, even. If you manage to get out of those ropes, you can go back to huntin' uranium." He chuckled. "Fact is, if you'd stuck to your prospectin' instead of snoopin' around us you'd be a lot better off right now."

"Let's go, Brock," Tabor prompted again.

The leader of the rustlers knotted the reins loosely around the horns of Stormy's and Calico's saddles. Then he picked up a stick from the ground and whacked both horses sharply across the flanks.

"Hii-ee-yah!" he shouted, swinging his hat over his head.

With startled snorts, the mustang and the pinto galloped away. Their drumming hoofs raced off into the night, disappearing toward the narrow mouth of the canyon.

"They'll rip themselves on the barbed wire!" Ned protested.

"We took it down when we came in," Brock

138

answered. "Don't worry, those horses ain't goin' to stop until they get home."

"And that's not going to give us any too much time," Slim called. "Let's beat it." He and Brock climbed into the truck cab beside Tabor.

"Oh, yeah," Tabor called back to the two young people on the ground. "Since you know what's been going on, you might as well know that we—er, borrowed fifty or sixty head during the past two months, and—"

"Shut up, Tabor!" Brock commanded.

"What harm can it do now, Brock?" Slim gloated. "Just wish I could see their dads' faces when they learn how we've slickered them."

Then the truck ground into gear and rumbled off into the night. Ned craned his neck and watched until the lights disappeared out the narrow mouth of the canyon. Suddenly, Hidden Canyon was left in pitch darkness. Ned could barely see Julie, who lay only three feet away.

"Ne-Ned," she said, "I'm afraid—really afraid."

"Don't be," Ned consoled. "They were right about one thing. Stormy and Calico will gallop all the way home. As soon as they arrive with empty saddles, everyone will come out hunting for us."

"But our fathers are in Mesa City," Julie reminded him. "They're not even due back home until tomorrow."

Ned had forgotten about that. "Now, don't worry, Julie," he said again, although he felt a little less confident. "Our mothers will know what to do. Being afraid can only make things worse."

"Oh, they couldn't be much worse, Ned," Julie sobbed.

"Sure they could be worse," Ned insisted. "A lot worse. We're not hurt. And we're not going to be."

"But those rustlers are going to get away, Ned."

"Don't worry, they'll be caught someday."

"Sure, but that may be too late to save the Box N, or the Rafter B, for that matter."

"Julie," Ned said, "let's not think about it right now. Let's see if we can work our way

140

out of these ropes." Wiggling along the ground, he inched over to her. "Let's see if we can sit back to back," he went on. "Maybe I can get my fingers on the knot near your wrists, and get you untied."

Both of them had been left leaning against the bank with their ankles bound and their hands tied behind them. With careful maneuvering, Ned finally was able to reach the ropes binding Julie's hands and feet. He was nearly exhausted by the time his groping fingers located a knot. Blindly, he picked at it until his fingers were tender and sore.

"Can't you undo it, Ned?" Julie asked anxiously.

"I—I can't even budge it," Ned said dismally. "That Tabor tied it awfully tight."

"Let me try yours," Julie said, wiggling around until she could touch the knot binding Ned's hands. For what seemed ages, Ned felt her plucking and tugging at the rope.

"It—it just won't work," Julie finally said in despair. Ned felt her slip back to the ground, panting with the exertion. "Ned, I hurt. These ropes are so tight. And it's getting cold. Oh, Ned, what are we going to do?"

It was a question that Ned had been asking himself. And now, in the darkness with a long night ahead of them, an answer was urgent. So many things could happen before they might be found by a searching party. The thought hadn't really frightened him before, but now, lying flat on the ground, helplessly bound hand and foot, the fear that he had kept trying to crowd back surged forward despite his strongest efforts against it.

"What can we do, Ned?" Julie asked again, through teeth which she was unable to keep from chattering.

"I don't know, Julie," Ned said soberly, although he hoped that Julie didn't sense his real fear. "I—I just don't know."

CHAPTER NINE

Manuel Machado had just finished bedding down his flock of sheep. He had brushed his teeth and washed up with water from his canteen. He had no more than settled into his bedroll under a cottonwood tree, when he heard the sound of a motor in the distance. He had no doubt that the noise came from the truck he had seen shuttling back and forth toward Mesa City several times during the past weeks.

In fact, Manuel had been giving quite a bit of thought to that truck. He had become convinced that it was the only one in the area. He also felt sure it was the one which had run into his flock that dark night.

So, right now, there was more than passing interest in Manuel's mind as he listened to the growling engine in the distance. By the time he caught his first glimpse of the headlights, Manuel saw that the driver was steering a winding course along the narrow ravine that sliced through the rangeland.

During the past few days Manuel had noticed other tire tracks crisscrossing the mesa or following the bottoms of the arroyos. It was apparent that the truckmen knew the country well, and had been doing much driving around.

For a few moments Manuel sat up in his bedroll located on the upper rim of the ravine. He watched the lights as the truck seemed to be feeling its way along. Then he saw the lights reflect from the walls of the narrow canyon. The truck picked up speed as the canyon widened and the wheels found solid traction on the packed dry sand and gravel of the canyon floor.

Then, with a frightening realization, Manuel scrambled out of his bedroll. He had bedded his sheep down in the bottom of the ravine, where they were well sheltered from the night breeze.

"Chico!" he called.

Obediently, the dog bounded up the bank from where he had been standing guard over the flock.

Startled by the sudden commotion, the sheep scrambled to their feet, bleating loudly. Within a few seconds they began milling nervously around in the bottom of the arroyo. Their sharp hoofs stirred up the sandy ground. Manuel coughed in the rising cloud of dust. Now he could neither see nor hear the truck.

"Chico, run them up the bank," Manuel shouted, sliding down the sandy bluff and working his way around to the far side of the flock. The dog ran back and forth, barking and nipping. Desperately, as he knew the truck would soon come rushing around the nearby bend in the canyon, Manuel waved his hat and yelled at the top of his lungs. Finally the lead ram headed for the slanting path which the flock had followed earlier to get down into the ravine.

Taking the ram's cue, the rest of the flock fell in behind. Both Chico and Manuel kept crowding them upward until the last sheep was safely on the mesa overlooking the ravine.

"Good boy, Chico." Manuel reached down and patted his loyal dog as the dust from the churned ground began to settle. "Come on. We'd better get out of the way ourselves," he added.

He followed Chico up the path, slipping and sliding in the loose dirt. When he reached the upper edge of the narrow canyon, he looked back. The truck lights drew closer, as the driver steered his course carefully through and around the scattered rocks and the bushes that grew in the bottom of the ravine.

Anger welled deep inside of Manuel as he watched the truck rumbling closer. He thought of what might have happened if he hadn't gotten the sheep out of the way in time.

Then the truck was close enough for

Manuel to see a jack rabbit spring out from in front of the headlights. It ran ahead of the truck for a ways, then scrambled frantically up the arroyo wall to safety.

As the truck drew opposite him, the young herder hugged the ground in order not to be caught in the reflection from the headlights. The bluff on which he lay was only a few feet higher than the top of the truck.

Then, as the truck reached the spot from which Manuel had just driven the sheep, it jammed to an abrupt stop. The driver raced the engine. The grinding clash of gears echoed down the arroyo. In the dim glow from the taillight, Manuel saw the rear wheels spinning a hole in the sandy soil.

"Hold it!" someone yelled above the roar of the motor. "You're spinnin' those wheels right down to the axle!"

The roar of the engine let up as the driver eased off on the throttle. Lying on his stomach and looking down, Manuel couldn't help but smile as he saw that the truck was already hopelessly stuck. It served them right, he thought, for running into his sheep that night.

The idea occurred to him that he might be able to sneak around behind the truck and get its license number. He wasn't at all anxious to meet the men in person. There was no telling what kind of men they might be. People who would run into a flock of sheep were better avoided.

Soon flashlight beams were probing around the truck.

"There's been goats or somethin' around here." The words floated up to Manuel. "They've got this ground all churned up and soft as oatmeal. No wonder the tires sank in."

"We've got to get out of here," another voice said urgently. "You two shove. I'll see if I can rock it."

There followed more grinding of gears and loud shouts from the men, but it seemed to Manuel that the tires simply dug themselves deeper into the ground.

"I told you we should have stayed up on the high ground, Brock," the driver said, after switching off the engine and climbing down from the cab.

"We were doing all right in this ravine,"

another replied, "until we hit this soft spot."

"Well," a third voice spoke up, "we can't just sit here. Get them horses out of the back and rope them to the bumper."

For the next ten minutes Manuel watched in amazement as the men opened the rear doors of the big square truck and brought out three horses. Quickly the men saddled them up. Then they stretched lariats from the saddle horns to the front bumper of the truck.

But even the strength of the horses added to the racing engine couldn't free the truck from the deep holes the rear wheels had spun into the ground.

"We're in a fine fix now," one of the men said angrily. "Now what brainstorm have you got, Brock?"

It was at that moment that one of the sheep bleated behind Manuel.

"Hey, what was that?" one of the men said quickly.

"Sounded like a sheep. Must be some up on that mesa. Might be a herder up there, too. Maybe he can give us some help. Hello, up there!"

149

Manuel cringed back. His first thought was that he didn't want to have anything to do with the men and that truck. Anyone who would run into his flock of sheep didn't deserve any help.

Then another thought came to him. Perhaps if he could help the men free their truck, they might be willing to pay for the earlier damage.

Besides, although it was strange that they had the habit of driving their truck around after dark, he had no real reason to fear them.

Chico began to growl as the men climbed up toward him. His hair stood up stiff on the back of his neck. Manuel rose to his feet just as one of the flashlight beams swept toward him and stopped.

"Hey, it's a kid," the voice behind the blinding light said. "He ain't gonna be much help."

"Come on down, kid," another of the trio invited calmly. "We've got ourselves in a little trouble down here. Your pa or someone with you?"

150

"Nope," Manuel said. He felt more at ease now. The men seemed friendly enough. "I'm tending the flock. Me and Chico, that is. Did you run into some of my sheep a week or so ago?" he asked bluntly.

"Run into your sheep?" the man whom Manuel had singled out as the one called Brock said. "Now, do we look like guys who would do such a thing, and then run off without payin' for the damage?"

Something in the way the man spoke made Manuel certain that they were the guilty men. Besides, he hadn't said a word about anyone running off without paying for the damage, although he had been about to mention it.

"Quit wasting time with the kid, Brock," one of the others said impatiently. "He can't help us none. And we ain't got no time to waste."

"You let me do the talkin', Slim," Brock commanded.

Manuel had quieted Chico. He moved on down to the truck. He stood looking at the wheels sunk deep in the soft sand.

"Boy, you sure are dug in," he said.

"We wouldn't have been if your blasted sheep—"

"Cut it, Tabor," Brock said sharply. "What's done is done, ain't it, kid?"

Manuel said, "I sure can't figure why you would be driving down this arroyo at night. I just did get my sheep out of the way in time."

"Now, kid," Brock said soothingly, "we wouldn't have run into your sheep."

"You did the other night."

"You seem mighty sure it was us," the tall man said sharply. "We don't own the only truck in this country, you know."

"Anyway," Brock said, "whether we did or not, we'll pay for the damage if you can help us get out of here. Are there any ranches around here where we might get someone with a truck or somethin' to help tug us out?"

"Sure," Manuel said, "there are several ranches."

"How far?"

"Three or four miles, I guess."

"O.K., good," Brock said. "You want to earn yourself ten dollars?"

Ten dollars? That was an awful lot of money.

"All you got to do is take us close enough to some ranch to see its lights. We'll take care of things from there on, and the ten dollars is yours."

"What's the idea, Brock?" Slim asked.

"We can't find our way to any ranches in this pitch blackness," Brock said. "If this young sheepherder knows his way, he can point out one of the ranches to us. It's that simple. Get it?"

"I get it," the fat man said. "Good idea, Brock." In the glow of the headlights Manuel saw his knowing grin. He also saw the metallic glint of a revolver butt stuffed in the man's waistband.

Suddenly it was all very clear why these men wanted him to point out a ranch house to them. They would get help, all right—at the point of a gun. As sure as he felt that, he felt just as sure that these men were criminals of some kind.

153

The realization sent a cold chill along Manuel's spine. It didn't matter what kind of criminals they were. It didn't even matter what reason they had for being in such a hurry to get their truck out of that part of the country. There were lots of loose ends that Manuel didn't understand. But the one thing he knew for sure was that he didn't want to help these men. Not for ten dollars, or anything else.

"How about it, kid?" Brock prompted. "You gonna show us to a ranch house or not?"

It was more of a threat than a question, but Manuel pretended not to notice the difference. He hoped the three men wouldn't guess that he had become suspicious.

"Four of us can't very well ride three horses," Manuel said.

"Tabor can stay here with the truck," Slim said. "He doesn't like to ride much, anyway. Too fat. All right, let's get going."

Manuel knew there was little chance to back out. He didn't know what the men were up to, but he was firmly convinced that it was something very dishonest.

154

"Which horse shall I ride?" he asked. But, even as he spoke, he moved automatically toward the roan gelding that stood farthest in the shadows away from the truck's headlights. It was more the location than the horse that interested Manuel. For a plan was forming in the young herder's mind.

"You can ride that roan if you want," Brock said. "You'll have to shorten the stirrups, though."

Moving slowly, almost carelessly, so as not to arouse suspicion, Manuel unlooped the lariat that stretched from the saddle horn to the bumper of the truck. He coiled it up. Then, trying to keep his hands from shaking with the excitement that filled him, he shortened the stirrup straps. All the while he kept the men in view out of the corner of his eye. They stood beside the truck, talking rapidly among themselves. Manuel couldn't hear what they said. But it really didn't matter.

What did matter was that they didn't seem to be paying any attention to him. Cautiously, he edged the roan farther and farther from the cone of light made by the truck head lamps. Manuel kept fumbling with the stirrup strap on the far side of the horse, although he had already adjusted it.

It wasn't until he actually stepped a foot into the stirrup that the men took sudden notice of him.

"Hey, kid," Brock commanded, "don't be in such a hurry to—"

But Manuel was set. He vaulted into the saddle, then ducked down low on the side farthest from the men.

"Yoww-ww!" he shouted, slapping the roan sharply on the flank.

"Hey!"

"Get him!"

"Stop or I'll shoot!"

But Manuel had planned his move well. By the time the men fully realized what was happening, Manuel had reined the horse in the opposite direction, putting the truck between the men and himself.

As the roan broke into a full gallop, two shots exploded into the night. But the bullets whined harmlessly overhead, as the welcome

156

darkness closed in around the galloping roan.

Manuel rode hard for about a half mile. Then he reined the horse to a stop. He sat for a moment, listening for following hoof-beats. No sound came to him.

"O.K., we better take it a little slower," he said, patting the roan's neck. "Don't want you stumbling in a prairie-dog burrow or some-thing. Besides, it's not going to be easy finding our way in this darkness."

Despite the darkness, there were enough familiar landmarks dimly visible against the sky for Manuel to keep a fairly direct course toward the Rafter B. He chose the Rafter B simply because it was the closest ranch.

It was nearly a half hour later that he caught his first glimpse of the lighted windows of the Rafter B ranch house. He reined to the left and angled across the mesa until he came to the dirt road that wound from the ranch across the flatland toward Mesa City. Once on the road, Manuel slacked off on the reins. The roan broke into a gallop on the solid footing of the road.

Manuel had just ridden under the rough log archway, when he spotted a lantern moving around outside the ranch house.

"Hello-o!" he called.

"Ned?" a woman's voice called anxiously. "Ned, is that you?"

Then Manuel was reining to a stop in the circle of lantern light.

"I'm Manuel Machado, Mrs. Bryant," he announced as he slid out of the saddle.

"Yes, Manuel," Ned's mother said. "Didn't I see you out here talking to Ned earlier today?"

"Yes, ma'am," the young herder said. "Is Mr. Bryant here?"

"He's in Mesa City, Manuel," the rancher's wife said. Her eyes seemed to be searching in the darkness. "Manuel, do you know where Ned is?"

"Ned? Isn't he here, either?"

"No. And I'm real worried."

"But we were together just this afternoon, Mrs. Bryant," Manuel said. "He and Julie and I—"

158

"Was Julie with him, too?"

"Yes, ma'am," Manuel said. "They're probably both over at Julie's right now."

"I—I don't think so," Mrs. Bryant said. "I don't think either of them is there. It's very late. Here come some headlights from the direction of the Box N now." She pointed toward the twin dots of light bobbing toward them. Obviously the car was racing as fast as possible along the rutted dirt road.

"Manuel," Mrs. Bryant said tensely, "something has happened to Ned and Julie. I feel it."

"But, Mrs. Bryant," Manuel said, puzzled, "how— why—"

"Ned was always very careful about Stormy," the ranchwoman said. "He would never have let Stormy run away and leave him stranded. And, above all, he would never have gotten out of the saddle and left the reins looped over the saddle horn."

Then, as Manuel's eyes became more accustomed to the flickering lantern light, the reason for Mrs. Bryant's words was all too

159

clear. At the nearby watering trough, with the white foam of sweat crusting his sleek blackness, stood Ned's horse, Stormy.

Manuel stared with speechless fright at the empty saddle.

CHAPTER TEN

Ned didn't know how long he had been asleep. He didn't even remember having dozed off. For over an hour he and Julie had tried unsuccessfully to work their knots loose. They had finally given up and lay quiet—thinking, talking, listening.

Then the coldness of the night had settled down around them. Both had started to shiver. They had listened to the distant sharp-pitched yapping of coyotes. Julie had shuddered, but the sound of coyotes didn't bother Ned. He had never heard of anyone being attacked by them. Wolves might have been a different matter, but in that part of the country wolves were quite rare.

He and Julie had talked for an hour or so. They had tried to keep fairly cheerful by assuring each other that someone would be out searching for them in a very few hours.

Ned hadn't wanted to admit the possibility of no one coming to look for them in Hidden Canyon until it was too late. He hadn't mentioned to Julie what might happen if neither Stormy nor Calico went straight back to the ranches. In stories and movies, horses ran directly back to their home corrals, and Ned had tried to make Julie believe this, but he knew that in real life the horse was just as apt as not to stop if it found decent grazing, or to head for water. Or it might just wander around for days enjoying its freedom before ending up back at the ranch. If that happened with Stormy and Calico, he and Julie were in a very dangerous plight.

But Ned had talked about other things. Julie added her ideas. Finally Ned had realized that he was doing all of the talking. He

162

twisted around and glanced at Julie where she lay huddled against the dirt embankment. Even though it was quite dark, he could see her face. Here eyes were closed. She had fallen asleep. He stopped talking. He leaned back against the ground and tried to make himself as comfortable as the binding ropes would allow. The events of the past few hours had exhausted him, and he must have fallen asleep almost immediately.

But he was awake now. It was still dark, although he saw faint traces of gray along the eastern horizon. Full dawn was not far off. It meant that he had been asleep for several hours. He tried to roll over to see Julie. Every muscle and bone in his body ached with cold and stiffness when he moved. After several painful efforts, he managed to flip over. Julie was still asleep, although shivering.

"Julie," Ned spoke softly in order not to startle her. In the gray reflection of coming dawn he saw her eyes flutter open.

"Brr-rr, Ned," she spoke through chattering teeth. "I'm so cold."

"How come you could feel it," he said,

163

trying to sound cheerful. "You've been sound asleep."

"Not all of the time, Ned," Julie replied. "I woke up several times. You were the one who was asleep. But why did you wake me up? I was more comfortable asleep."

"It's nearly dawn," Ned said. "We'd better start figuring out some way to get loose or—"

"Ned!" Julie tensed suddenly. "Shh-h! Listen!"

After waiting a few seconds Ned said, "I don't hear anything. Maybe it was just your teeth chattering."

"Don't try to be funny, Ned," Julie scolded. "I thought I heard a shout."

Ned saw that she was serious. He listened intently.

Then it came again. This time there was no mistake.

"Hear it?" Julie asked anxiously.

"I sure did!" Ned said, struggling to straighten up.

"Ne-ed! Ju-lie-ee!" They were long-drawn-out shouts. Neither a man's nor a woman's voice.

164

"It's Manuel!" Julie said quickly. "Manuel! Manuel!" she called.

Ned began to shout also. They kept it up until they heard the clop, clop, clop of running hoofs approaching. Then Manuel appeared at the top of the bluff over their heads. He grinned down at them through the gray dawn. Ned recognized the roan he was riding as one of the horses belonging to the rustlers. Manuel was leading Stormy and Calico behind him.

"Hi, you all right?" he greeted them.

"Yes," Julie cried gleefully. "Boy, are we glad to see you, Manuel!"

"You sure picked a funny place to camp for the night," the Mexican boy said, guiding the horses down the sloping part of the bluff.

"Forget the jokes," Ned said, "and get us loose."

Slipping from his saddle, Manuel pulled his hunting knife from its leather sheath. He knelt beside Julie and quickly cut her free. Then he cut the ropes binding Ned. The two young people got to their feet slowly, lamely.

165

They started exercising the soreness and stiffness out of their muscles and joints.

"Boy, oh, boy," Ned said, "what a night!"

"Manuel," Julie said finally, "how did you ever find us way out here?"

"Just lucky, I guess," the Mexican boy said. "And, besides, I did some praying. But I figured this was as good a place as any to look after not finding you in Wild Horse Canyon."

"Wild Horse Canyon?" Ned said. "How long have you been looking for us, Manuel?"

"Since about midnight, I guess."

"Where'd you get that roan?" Julie asked. "It looks like one that those—those rustlers had."

"Rustlers?" Manuel said. "Is that what those three fellows with the truck have been doing?"

"Didn't you know?" Ned said. "No, I guess you wouldn't, at that. Well, they're rustlers, all right. Julie and I can tell you all about that. And when we catch them—"

"That shouldn't be too hard," Manuel said, smiling.

"What do you mean?" Julie asked.

166

"It's a pretty long story," the young sheep-herder said. "But we'd better get going, if you feel like riding. I can tell you on the way."

Soon Julie and Ned had worked away their stiffness and cold. They swung into their saddles. It was now fully light, although the sun had not yet come up.

"Follow me," Manuel instructed.

"Follow you?" Ned said. "We know our way to the ranch."

"Hey, don't go that way," Julie said, as Manuel started to ride off. "That's not the way back home. And I'm hungry."

"I thought maybe you wanted to see if those rustlers are caught yet," Manuel said.

"We do," Ned said, "but—"

"Then come on," the Mexican boy prompted. "There will be plenty of time to eat later."

As they loped side by side across the mesa, Manuel told them the story of the night's happenings. He told them everything that took place from the time he first saw the truck lights probing their way down the arroyo until he had ridden up to the Rafter B Ranch

"I thought maybe you wanted to see if those rustlers are caught."

and seen Stormy standing at the watering trough, empty-saddled.

"And when your mother arrived, Julie," Manuel went on, "she said that Calico had come straight home, too. Boy, I'll tell you, your mothers are both plenty worried."

"Where are they now?" Julie asked.

"Ned's mother drove into town to get your fathers and the sheriff. Julie, your mother took the jeep and headed for some of the other ranches to round up the neighbors. They're probably getting together some search parties right about now."

"And you came looking for us," Julie finished.

"Well, I know this country pretty well," Manuel said, smiling. "A sheepherder covers a lot of ground and has plenty of time to look things over. I figured you'd be pretty close to Wild Horse Canyon or here, so I led Stormy, went to your place and got Calico, and started out."

"Lucky for us you figured that way," Ned said.

"You didn't need to worry," Manuel said

modestly. "If I arrived back at the truck without you, the plan was for everyone to start out in a big search for you."

"Is that where we're heading," Julie asked, "the truck?"

"Yep."

"What if those guys got the truck out on hard ground again?" Ned wondered.

"Not a chance," Manuel assured him. "It's clear down to the axles."

"But they still had two horses," Julie replied. "I'll bet they beat it as soon as you got away."

"Maybe so," Manuel admitted. "But I don't think they will get very far, not with the sheriff's posse all over the place. Besides, there were only two horses for the three of them. One guy was pretty fat, too."

"Yeah, we know," Ned said. "His name was Tabor."

"Boy," Julie said, "our uranium hunt sure turned into something, didn't it, Ned?"

"Uranium?" Ned said suddenly. "Jeepers, we forgot and left the Geiger counter back there in Hidden Canyon!"

"We can get it later," Julie said.

"Look, there's the truck," Manuel announced. He reined the roan to a stop at the edge of the arroyo and pointed below and ahead.

The dusty brown truck was still stuck deep in the soft earth. Several cars and jeeps were parked near the edge of the small, winding canyon. From the distance, it seemed that some twenty or thirty people were gathered around the truck.

The three young people began yelling as they rode at full gallop toward the scene.

The small crowd greeted them happily as they reined to a stop and slid from their saddles. After embracing their parents and answering a few quick questions, Ned and Julie looked around for the three rustlers.

"They were gone when we got here," Ned's father explained. "The tracks showed that they left on the two horses."

"But, Dad," Ned said anxiously, "we've got to catch them. They've been rustling our cattle and—"

"They won't get far, son," Mrs. Bryant

assured him. "The whole sheriff's posse is out tracking them now. With two men on one horse, they're not going to travel very fast."

"The rest of us stayed here," Julie's father explained. "If Manuel hadn't brought you in within the next fifteen minutes, we were all set to search the whole countryside with a fine-toothed comb. Now that you're safe, though, I guess the rest of us had better go help the posse."

But that proved unnecessary. Mr. Nelson had barely finished talking when a large group of horsemen appeared coming up the arroyo. As they drew closer, Ned saw the three sober-faced rustlers at the front of the group. Slim and Brock were astride one horse, Tabor slumped in the saddle of the second.

All three had their hands tied behind their backs.

CHAPTER ELEVEN

The posse rode up and stopped in front of the waiting group.

"Well," Sheriff Kincaid said, "hunting's been mighty good this morning. Glad to see you youngsters safe," he added, turning to Julie and Ned. "As for these three *hombres,* they were as easy to track as snakes in soft sand. Didn't have any trouble getting 'em to confess, either."

The three solemn captives took turns glowering at Ned and Julie.

Brock said, "We sure never figured to get taken in by three punk kids."

"Doesn't surprise me a bit," Sheriff Kincaid said sharply. "Seems to me that these three young people are a good deal smarter than you crooks."

"I have no doubt about it," Ned's father said, looking proudly at Ned and Julie and Manuel.

"Well, I'd better get these fellows behind bars where they belong," Sheriff Kincaid said. "We'll take 'em in the truck. Mr. Bryant, wonder if you'd mind holding their three horses out at the Rafter B for a couple of days until we can come and get them? The livery stable in town is pretty full."

"Sure," Ned's father said. "Nelson and I will take them out to the ranch."

Soon the truck was pushed and towed out onto solid ground. They locked the three rustlers in the back. One of the sheriff's deputies got in and started driving it toward the highway that led to Mesa City.

"Oh, that reminds me," Sheriff Kincaid said, as he prepared to start back to town. "There may be a reward on those three birds. If there is, it belongs to you youngsters."

174

The thought of how some reward money might help make up for the lost Rafter B and Box N cattle delighted Ned. Yet another thought crowded quickly into his head.

"If there's any reward," Julie put the very same thought into words, "it belongs to our friend, Manuel."

"That's right," Ned said. "If it hadn't been for Manuel— Hey, Manuel, where are you going?"

The young Mexican boy had slid out of the saddle and was making his way up the side of the arroyo. "I have to check my sheep," he called.

"Will you come right back?"

"Sure," he said, smiling, "if you want me to."

"We do," Julie assured him.

Soon the truck and the posse left. The neighbors who had come to aid in the search said good-by and moved off toward their various ranches. Finally, only Ned and Julie and their parents remained.

"I imagine you children are starving," Ned's mother said.

"I could eat a jack rabbit," Julie said.

"Well, you children come with us in the pickup," Mrs. Nelson said. "The men can lead the horses back to the ranch."

Unlike Julie, Ned wasn't very hungry at the moment. His mind was filled with too many things. "Dad," he asked, "will those rustlers have to pay for the cattle they stole?"

"I'm afraid it doesn't work quite that way, Ned," Mr. Bryant said. "They will be sent to prison to pay for their crimes. But crooks don't usually pay their debts—except to society. After all, the cattle are butchered and gone."

"Then we're not much better off than before, are we?" Julie asked.

"Oh, yes, we're much better off," Mr. Nelson put in. "We're rid of the rustlers. Now the ranchers around here won't have any more trouble with missing cattle."

"But what about us?" Julie wondered. "Are—are we still going to have to move away from the Box N?"

"You knew about that?" Mr. Nelson asked, surprised.

"I—I heard you and mother talking one night," Julie admitted.

"Well, I don't know," Mr. Nelson said. "That's what Mr. Bryant and I went to Mesa City to see about. We weren't having much luck with the bank. But things may be a little different now that the rustlers won't be bothering us. We just don't know yet."

"Dad," Ned asked, "is it the same with us at the Rafter B?"

"Both ranches are pretty much in the same boat, son," Ned's father said. "I guess there's no point in hiding it from you children any longer. You have proved yourselves to be pretty grown up. The big trouble right now is that we have almost no cattle left. You can't operate a ranch without a herd."

"We'll get more cattle," Julie said eagerly. "We'll start new herds."

"Wish it were that easy," her father said. "Cattle cost money. That's the second thing we seem to be short on. But don't you kids start worrying. We haven't given up hope, and we haven't stopped working. And, after all, didn't you say there were several head of our cattle out in Hidden Canyon?"

"That's right," Ned said. "I almost forgot. There are the cattle the rustlers left when we spoiled their game."

"You mean when we dropped in," Julie added, laughing. "Manuel said there were eight head—three with the Box N brand and five with the Rafter B."

"Well, that's eight we wouldn't have had if you kids hadn't been on the job," Mr. Bryant said.

"But don't you two ever get into anything like that again," Ned's mother scolded. "You had us worried to death."

"Don't worry, Mom," Ned promised, "we won't—not if we can help it."

"I'll say not," Julie confirmed.

"We'd better be starting home," Mrs. Nelson suggested.

"You go ahead," Mr. Bryant said. "Nelson and I will ride out and bring those cattle in."

"Good idea," Julie's father said. "I'd also like to get a look at how those rustlers were operating."

178

"May Ned and I go, too?" Julie asked.

"But you're both so hungry, and—"

"Oh, but I feel fine," Ned said. "Besides, we left the Geiger counter out in Hidden Canyon. We want to get it."

Just then Manuel scrambled back down the edge of the arroyo. "Chico is taking good care of the sheep," he announced, grinning.

"We have the extra horses, Manuel," Ned said. "How about riding back out to Hidden Canyon with us?"

"Oh, I'd like that," the Mexican boy said.

"Now, Children," Mrs. Bryant protested, "I don't think you should—"

"I believe it will be all right if they go." Mr. Bryant spoke up in their behalf. "After all, they were in on this business from the beginning. They deserve to see it through if they want to. We won't be long. Too bad about your uranium prospecting, though," he consoled. "Guess you kids got more than you bargained for—and not uranium, either."

"Oh, we can try again sometime," Ned said. "Prospecting, that is. I still think there must be uranium around here someplace."

179

Mounting up, the two men and the three young people soon rode away. The two mothers shook their heads, and drove off toward the ranches.

A while later, after looking over the abandoned camp site in Wild Horse Canyon, the group remounted and rode to Hidden Canyon.

"Those fellows sure had it figured out," Mr. Bryant said, after surveying the scene in Hidden Canyon. "Looks like they rounded up the cattle during the day and hid them here or in Wild Horse Canyon. Probably used Wild Horse Canyon until you children showed up. After that, they doubtless figured it would be safer to move their operations over here. They couldn't be sure you had fallen for their claim of being uranium prospectors."

"But if they were suspicious of us," Julie said, "why didn't they leave here entirely?"

"Greed is a strange thing, Julie," Mr. Nelson said. "Greedy and dishonest people just don't think very straight. Well, I guess we've seen about everything here. Might as well get started back. I'll go get those steers."

"Make it easier if I go with you," Ned's father said. "You kids can go hunt up your Geiger counter. We'll be right back with the cattle." The two fathers turned and rode up toward the dead end of the canyon, where the eight cattle were still in sight, grazing on the sparse grass.

"Where did you leave your Geiger counter?" Manuel asked. "I didn't notice it this morning."

"It's not far from where you found us," Ned said. "One of the men put it on the ground, but it was pretty dark, so I don't know just where."

"We shouldn't have much trouble finding it, though," Julie said. "There are a lot of rocks around. It's probably behind one."

"Well, let's go look," Manuel said eagerly.

"Maybe we should just leave it," Julie said, smiling wanly. "Ever since we started out looking for uranium, all we've had is trouble."

"You don't mean that, Julie," Ned said.

181

"Besides, if it hadn't been for the Geiger counter we never would have come across those rustlers. And goodness knows when they would have been caught."

"I guess you're right," Julie admitted. "Anyway, we got a few steers back. But I'm still worried."

"What about?" Ned asked.

"About the Box N—about having to move, and—"

"Worrying won't do any good, Julie," Manuel said.

"That's right," Ned agreed, although he had been doing quite a bit of worrying himself. "Something will work out. We'll both have new herds of cattle before long. Wait and see."

He hoped he sounded convincing, even though he wasn't convinced himself. It took more than talk and wishing to get a new herd started. Mostly, it took money. And where was money going to come from?

"That looks like the place," Julie said suddenly. She pointed to the low, steeply sloping section of the bluff where she and Ned had tumbled down the night before.

"Boy, it sure is rocky," Manuel exclaimed. "I didn't notice it this morning. Guess I was too happy finding you to notice. It's a wonder you two weren't really hurt."

"Oh, I banged my shoulder a couple of times," Ned said. "But I didn't notice it was so rocky, either. Hey, there it is. There's the Geiger counter."

The three of them slid out of their saddles and walked the few remaining yards to the foot of the bluff. Ned picked up the counter and slipped the strap around his shoulder.

"Doesn't look like it's hurt any," he said, inspecting the black box carefully. "I'd better check the battery."

"You can do that later, Ned," Julie said. "We have to get back to meet our fathers. There they come with the cattle now."

But Ned already had flicked the switch of the Geiger counter. He held the phones up to his ears to listen for the background count. "It seems O.K.," he said.

183

Noting the formation of rocks that made up a large part of the crumbling bluff, he started wandering back and forth among them.

"You just won't give up, will you, Ned," Julie scolded mildly.

"Well," Ned said, "some of these rocks have a greenish-yellow tinge to them. I've read that uranium ore often looks like that. Anyway, it won't hurt to find out. After all, it may be a long time before we get out this way again."

"That's all right with me," Julie said. "Things are more peaceful around home, anyway."

For the next couple of minutes Ned concentrated on the rocks. No unusual noises came from the Geiger counter. He saw his father and Mr. Nelson coming closer with the cattle. He was about to switch off the counter, when he came to a sharp bend in the canyon. It was caused by a jutting wall of rock, which had refused to wash away like so much of the surrounding soil.

Ned walked along the foot of the rugged face of rock, waving the probe of the counter over its rough surface. Suddenly he stopped

184

and listened. His eyes opened wide. Then he whirled around and began shouting at the top of his lungs.

"Ned, where are you?" Julie called from the opposite side of the bend.

"Over here," Ned called back, stepping out so Julie and Manuel could see him. "Hurry up! Come here! Quick!"

"What's the matter, Ned?" Manuel asked anxiously, as he and Juie rushed over.

"Shh-h!" Ned held the headset to his ears. "Listen!"

"How can we listen when you've got the Geiger counter?" Julie asked. "Ned, you—you look so funny!"

"Julie! Manuel!" Ned exclaimed. "The clicks! They—they're real fast. Sounds like eggs frying in grease!"

"What does that mean?" Manuel asked innocently. "You hungry?"

Without bothering to answer, Ned continued passing the wandlike probe of the Geiger counter over the face of the rock cliff. In openmouthed amazement he listened to the rapid clicking in the earphones. Then he

185

looked down at the metal box and watched the needle of the dial jump wildly.

"Listen!" he said again, as Julie and Manuel crowded in close. Ned turned the earphones outward from his head in order that they could hear the close-spaced clicks.

"Boy, I hear it!" Manuel nodded eagerly.

"Ned," Julie said, "does—does that mean—"

"Wait a second," Ned interrupted. "I've got to make sure the counter isn't broken."

He ran a few yards out onto the sandy floor of the canyon. As soon as he was away from the rocks, the clicking dropped off to a normally slow background count. When he went back to the rocks, the counter once more began to click rapidly.

"Julie!" he yelled, satisfied now. "Manuel! We've found it! Uranium! Those rustlers led us right to uranium without even knowing it."

"Ned," Julie cried excitedly, "maybe we'll be able to get our new herds!"

"Sure, sure," Ned said. Then he looked at the Mexican boy, who seemed just as happy about it as he and Julie. "Manuel, you're in on this, too, you know. Want to be partners?"

186

"We've found it! Uranium!"

"You mean that, Ned?" The young Mexican sheepherder looked at him in disbelief.

"Sure, he means it," Julie put in. "After all, we're friends. If it hadn't been for you—"

"You can buy more sheep," Ned said, grinning. He no longer felt any hostility toward either the sheep or the sheepmen. In fact, he even admitted to himself that it had been a silly idea to begin with. Then he took a deep breath. "But maybe we shouldn't be counting our chickens before they're hatched."

"Or our uranium before it's dug," Julie added.

"But, boy," Ned went on, "if this Geiger counter is telling the truth—"

His words were interrupted by the loud drumming of hoofs on the ground. The three young people looked up to see Mr. Bryant and Mr. Nelson galloping hard toward them.

"Hey, what's the trouble?" Ned's father called anxiously as he reined his horse to a stop. "Why all the yelling and jumping around?"

"One of you get stung by a scorpion?"

Julie's father asked quickly, sliding from his saddle.

"Scorpion?" Julie laughed.

"Trouble?" Ned cried gleefully. "No trouble, Dad. Not any more! Here." He handed the Geiger counter to his father. "Listen, Dad, I think those clicks mean the end of our troubles!"

Then, while the two men looked on in amazement, Ned, Julie, and Manuel threw their arms around each other. Whooping like wild Indians, they began doing a dance on the sandy floor of Hidden Canyon.

END